M000309440

ORAM RED

ORAM RED

G.F. CURRY

ORAM RED
Copyright © 2021 by G.F. Curry

Cover photo by Pamela Keith
Cover design by Debbie Duffield

Printed in the United States of America

PeaPatch Publishing
428 Widgeon Cove
Fripp Island, SC 29920

LCCN: 2021914744
ISBN: 978-1-7373773-2-0

For my mother, Liane M. Curry

CONTENTS

Preface

The Triumph Nuclear Plant, situated on a small island on the Squankum River, is nestled between tall marsh grasses and many tidal creeks in Possum County, New Jersey, an area of small towns on the southern end of the Garden State in the Delaware Valley. The land at one time could only be accessed by boat and was enjoyed through the years as a prosperous hunting ground by Native Americans, Dutch, Swedes, British, and finally, by Americans after the Revolutionary War. It boasted a cornucopia of wild hogs, turkeys, quail, pheasants, and muskrats.

Except for the Triumph Nuclear Plant, not much is on the island. Surrounding the island are many small towns, farm land, and marshes.

The many tributaries surrounding the island boasted bountiful harvests of crab, shad, and sturgeon. Much like the California Gold Rush in the Wild West, little villages along this part of the Squankum River flourished after the Civil War until the mid-1930s. Rail service, post offices, canning and processing plants, restaurants, and schools popped up everywhere. The precious caviar from the sturgeon was shipped to the finest restaurants in the world. Everyone in these towns prospered until the sturgeon disappeared due to overfishing and lack of proper wildlife management.

Many once prosperous villages turned into ghost towns and eventually dust. Some residents stayed and made a living as baymen and fur trappers. Today, there are still a few of these Baymen still crabbing and trapping muskrats for fur. But most have other jobs to supplement their incomes. Most of these baymen are descendants of crabbers and trappers who lived in the area a hundred or more years ago. Some of the names can be found in history books for having served in the Revolutionary War as well as the Civil War. Possum County, indeed, is rich in American history.

A Strange County

The tiny island, has always been referred to by the locals as "The Island."

It's a beautiful place with a history. The county's nutrient-rich soil makes it one of the best agricultural areas in the country, producing some of the nation's finest tomatoes and corn.

The local farmers produce the best tomatoes and corn in the country.

But to an outsider, this is a strange and different place.

Here is where the strange begins.

First of all, it's named "Possum County," not the proper spelling of "opossum" but that's not the strange part. Even though there may be an occasional opossum running around, this place is loaded with muskrats.

Yes, muskrats. The locals worship the muskrat.

There is an annual Muskrat Festival complete with a Muskrat Queen competition where the lucky young lady gets to ride on a fire truck in the annual Muskrat Parade.

Firefighters from the local fire departments get together and harvest a massive amount of these "marsh rats" for their annual Muskrat Feast. They spend all night skinning and breading the mean-spirited creatures for a muskrat fry the next day. Tickets to the event sell out quickly every year. Yes, you read it correctly, a muskrat fry!

I know what you're thinking, do they taste like chicken?" Having never sampled a muskrat, I wouldn't know, however, those who attend the feast love them and encourage others to try them. I just can't seem to get up the courage to dine on rodents.

These "delicious creatures" are vegans and only eat the green roots of the marsh grass, which supposedly contributes to their clean taste. The muskrats get a tasty treat when the firefighters perform an annual controlled burn of the marsh grasses to encourage new growth.

Muskrats have been a reliable source of sustenance and clothing for residents for at least a couple of centuries.

Construction Begins

The Possum County Island was purchased by the Rising Sun Energy Corporation. The island eventually was expanded with a road instead of ferry service. The Rising Sun Energy Corporation's nuclear division was issued permits to build up to four nuclear reactors. Even though the island was small, as islands go, it still was big enough to provide room for the quartet of reactors. If all four had been built, the facility would have been the nation's largest nuclear complex. However, only one permit was used to build the Triumph No.1 plant. While plans were being made to build the other three plants, the political climate soured on nuclear energy due to a serious mishap at the Three Mile Island nuclear station. A moratorium was placed on building any new nuclear reactors.

The Triumph plant, which was a pressurized water reactor, featured a circulating water facility to draw water to cool the reactor from the Squankum River. The service water facility would transfer the slightly heated water back into the river. Meanwhile, during the construction of Triumph No. 1, a cooling tower had been completed in anticipation of building more units that also would have included two boiling water reactors (BWRs).

Triumph No. 1 featured one Westinghouse Reactor capable of 1169 Mega Watts (MW) output. Its 500 Kilo Volt (KV) lines can be heard crackling in the fog on a misty, fall morning. There were several buildings on site including a wastewater treatment building, turbine, radioactive waste facility, and auxiliary buildings as well as an administration building, maintenance shops, fire department, and warehouse. A fenced enclosure separates the switchyard from the rest of the plant. Outside the protected area was the security center as well as the processing center and plant parking lots.

The Island Shuffle

All Union labor was used to build the Triumph Nuclear plant.

This project employed and provided Union Workers of every craft from around the country with a very lucrative wage.

Shortly after high school graduation, my father presented me with an offer I could not refuse. The local union hall offered a special summer program for their members' children who were age eighteen and older. They would be placed on various construction sites within their respective territories as helpers for their working members.

As luck would have it, I wound up working on the new Triumph nuclear plant. Since my father worked elsewhere, he found a former co-worker who was kind enough to carpool with me and show me the ropes.

My carpool partner was Bobby O'Donnell.

He was a tough, mid-forties, corncob pipe-smoking American of Irish descent who came from a family of union electricians. They were a tough bunch of hardworking men that got the job done and whose reputation preceded them.

You did not want to piss these men off unless you wanted to wear your ass as a hat.

My name is Francis O'Dowd, aka "Franny."

I was one hundred and forty-eight pounds of skin and bones. After picking up Bobby to go to work, we'd make the trek to The Island picking up our fried egg and cheese sandwiches from Harry's Country Store along the way. Traffic on the access road made you think you were heading to the Jersey shore in the summer. Bumper to bumper traffic into the parking lot.

Right before a bend in the road leading to the plant was a farmhouse with a pen that held a horse and a pig with the biggest balls I have ever seen. Every day, a cop parked outside the farm would stop traffic, motioning drivers with no or expired inspection stickers to pull over. I swear the company was in sync with this cop. If you didn't make it past him, you would be docked an hour for being late. Bobby and I had the timing down pat. Every day at 6:45 a.m. we would see him in our rear-view mirror stopping traffic.

Several thousand cars, trucks, and campers filled the parking lot of the construction site. License plates from all around the country could be seen. Men worked around the clock on three shifts. Overtime was available to anyone who desired it. Some men slept in their campers or took catnaps in their cars, then went right back to work.

Anything you wanted could be purchased in the parking lot from food, guns, and knives to haircuts and prostitutes. I particularly enjoyed the different styles of barbecue the boys from Virginia and North Carolina would bring up with them to sell.

After parking, we would line up in what the men called "cattle chutes." These were segregated by craft. We would line up in the chutes according to our trade. When the horn would blow, we would walk through and receive our "brass." Each person would get a quarter-size piece of brass with their employee number on it from the timekeeper. Upon leaving, you would toss your brass into a hopper as you rushed out at the end of the day.

Every morning while waiting in the cattle chute to get my brass, I would hear the delightful sounds of a harmonica playing over the loudspeakers to be followed by a very irate security supervisor yelling at the musician/guard to knock it off.

It just so happened, our harmonica-playing security guard left that job to go on to better things, becoming a star in a popular television series at the time.

He eventually became a famous movie star whose name was a household word.

Speaking of guards, they would line up alongside the cattle chutes at the end of the day looking for workers to stop and search for stolen tools. One Barney Fife like guard had his eye on me daily. This guy would choose to search me every time we made eye contact. I was short in stature compared to most of the men, so I would see him looking around for me to pull out of line. I guess because I was so young, he thought I was an easy target to harass.

To this day, that summer was the hottest of my life. What was worse than being covered in sweat were the greenhead flies biting the shit out of me. The only nice thing about those flies was the satisfaction of smashing them between your hands. They were teeth with wings; however, they flew slowly and were easy to kill. Just when you thought it was unbearable, the cool breeze off the Squankum River would cease, leaving you in a cloud of nasty, biting, no-see-ums.

The Island 500

After a scorching hot day, I would meet up with Bobby to get ready to drop our brass and race to our car, getting a jump on the usual traffic jam. One particular week, Bobby had been excited for the weekend to come since it was the union's softball championship upstate and Bobby was their star player. Bobby was a foreman for a crew in a different area than where I worked. Bobby asked whether I could leave fifteen minutes earlier so we could get a jump on the traffic. He wanted to get home and on the road to the tournament upstate. I told him my foreman would never let me leave early and usually made sure I was the last to leave. He told me my responsibility as a helper was to make sure the crew's tools were put away and securely locked up. Bobby told me he would take care of that and I should be ready to leave fifteen minutes early.

The end of the day finally arrived. I was in the process of rolling up air hoses when I saw Bobby walk over to my foreman. Bobby then called me over. After explaining to my foreman that we carpooled and I needed to leave early so Bobby could make it to the tournament, the foreman told Bobby we should have driven separately. Not an especially tall man, but broad in the shoulders with a stocky build, Bobby, in one swift grab, pinned the foreman by his neck to the wall with his feet two feet off the ground. He yelled to Bobby, "Go ahead, take him, take him!"

As we started to leave, I glanced back at the foreman taking apart a water hose thinking it was an air hose.

The poor bastard wound up soaked from head to toe.

As we got close to the head of the line in the cattle chute, the horn blew, and we ran as fast as we could to my car. Bobby was ahead of me when he lost his balance. I saw him bounce off two parked cars in a huge cloud of dust and yell, "Fuck!" but we still kept running. We made it to the car, and I spun wheels as I raced toward the end of the road. As I was driving, I asked Bobby what happened? Up ahead, some men got out of a car and pushed another guy's stalled vehicle off the road and into the creek. Bobby said, "Just keep driving, and get me to the Well!"

When we got to the Well, a bar located within five minutes of the plant, Bobby bought our daily six-pack of Miller High Life to go along with a pickled egg. He asked owner Maggie McBride if she had a towel and ice. Bobby had broken his finger and it was dangling. He held his finger in place while Maggie wrapped his hand in ice and the towel. Maggie suggested he get to a hospital immediately. Bobby said, "Thanks for the ice, Maggie. I'm not going to miss this tournament for anything!"

I insisted on taking him to the emergency room. He told me to just take him home and his wife would take him to the hospital. I thought that was fair enough, and we cracked open our beers. Yes, we were drinking and driving. It was the norm back then and looking back, I'm not proud of it. I dropped off Bobby and heard him tell his wife, who happened to be in the yard, that they needed to get on the road. I said to myself, "What a tough dude". I hope one day I could be like that."

The following Monday morning I arrived to pick up Bobby at his home. I asked him if he made it to the tournament.

He replied, "No, my wife insisted on taking me to the E.R., I never made it to the game!" As I was telling him how sorry I was that he didn't make it, I noticed a cast on his arm and something weird about it.

I said, "Why is your hand positioned in the cast as if you were holding a beer?"

Bobby told me that since he drank beer using his right hand, he brought a can of beer with him so they could fit the cast around it. With a laugh, I thought to myself, "You just can't make this up."

Years Gone By

Years have come and gone since those sweltering days of my youth. My initial plans after high school were to become a music teacher/performer. I decided that going to college to be a music teacher wasn't going to pay for the lifestyle that I knew I someday wanted. I tried my hand at selling real estate and enjoyed that, but that too wouldn't satisfy my need to be working with my hands.

A couple of years had passed when I applied and was accepted into the IBEW (International Brotherhood of Electrical Workers) Inside Wireman Apprenticeship program.

After completing my apprenticeship, I spent time working for various contractors on roads, bridges, prisons, malls, and hospitals only to find a home in the nuclear industry.

A challenging and, most of the time, satisfying but certainly rewarding career.

I thought of Triumph as my own plant as did many of the other old-timers. Over the years I worked upgrading the security systems, main power transformers, motorized operated valves (MOVs), general maintenance, as well as design change packages (DCPS) and other refueling outage work. I was a fire watch (personnel who maintain surveillance of areas where welding and torch-cutting occur and where sparks have the potential of starting a fire) one day and eventually worked my way up to a general foreman supervisor until my retirement. I literally grew up in this plant.

Weird Events and Close Calls

Most close calls eventually disappeared with the wisdom of age and responsibility, however, there were still a few weird events and close calls.

We were working fourteen hours a day, seven days a week for months on end. I had spent most of my time working inside this massive, dome-shaped containment building. The containment building contains four steam generators and houses the nuclear reactor. The inside of the building was a steel vessel with an outside shell made up of four feet of concrete. This building was designed at the time to survive a direct crash by a 747-jumbo jet. There is a large cargo hatch with inside and outside removable covers. These covers are protected by a missile shield—concrete blocks several feet thick. Back in the day, the missile shields and the inner and outer hatches of the containment building were removed for refuel outage operations. Today the hatch is fitted with a thick steel insert that has smaller hatches for the transfer of equipment. Before then, the hatch was left wide open and, in this particular case, a great horned owl decided to soar into the containment hatch.

The owl must have chased a smaller bird into the hatch finally perching on the containment spray ring almost two hundred feet inside the reactor building. Eight-hour crews were changing shifts. I happened to be on a fourteen-hour shift working as temporary power and light (TP&L) outage support. Everyone by now had heard about the owl and I could see it on the spray ring several yards above the giant polar crane.

The local newspapers did a story on the bird and how it forced refuel outage operations to cease until the owl could be vacated from the building. Every day that bird was in the Containment Building, the company was losing millions. Every operation was on hold. The company had a dilemma on its hands since killing the bird was not an option. The media would have been all over the story, angering activists and bird lovers. Most recently Audubon experts had failed to remove the owl. Now it was him and me alone (I thought). Since I was curious about the creature, I had read the night before about how owls see images. They hyperfocus on their prey, which is how this big guy probably got into trouble. Thinking I was alone, against all procedures, I climbed the ladder of the giant polar crane to get a better look at the bird. My movement scared the bird, which flew to the top of one of the containment fan coil units (CFCU) just below the top of the polar crane. I shimmied down the ladder. Since it was a radiation / contamination area, I was dressed in full protective clothing. I grabbed a spare cloth bootie from Rad Pro (the radiation protection department). I filled the bootie with muslin cloth, tied it together with a rope, and positioned myself between the bird and the open hatch. As a child I remembered watching sadly as a red-tailed hawk snatched a dove while its mate circled in the air above making frantic sounds. Those sounds are forever etched in my mind. I decided to try something. I swung the roped bootie over my head, making that same frantic sound I remembered. After about five minutes, the owl started to ruffle his feathers. He dove toward me and I panicked and dropped the rope. The bird flew back to the top of the fan coil units. The bird didn't aim for the bootie, instead, it aimed for my hand. All of a sudden, I heard, "Damn, you almost got him!"

It was the containment coordinator. I was certain I was fired. Lucky for me, this guy wasn't your typical disgruntled "suck ass." He wasn't out to make a name for himself by firing workers for procedural violations. He happened to be an animal lover.

After I realized I wasn't going to be escorted out, I told him, "Yes, I will try this again, and when he dives at my hand, throw a lab coat on him."

All I can say was that I was young, dumb, and lucky.

The coordinator said he would, and looking back, I realize what a noble, but stupid act of kindness it was. That owl's talons were huge and sharp as a razor.

Once again, I spun the bootie around in the air, this time for ten minutes. I didn't hear a peep from the coordinator. The owl ruffled his feathers again as I asked the coordinator if he was still behind me.

He answered, "Yes!"

Within seconds, the bird dove, back flipped, and aimed those blades right at me.

A light breeze blew, and the owl's outstretched wings were about a foot short of the hatch on each side. In a split second, the bird flipped and flew out the hatch into the sunset.

"Wow, did you see that? He must have had a six foot or more wingspan," the coordinator said.

After a big hug, the coordinator introduced himself and asked my name and employee number.

"Oh, shit," I thought. Here we go. "I'll be shit-canned for sure."

I changed into my street clothes and returned to our daily muster area. It is a huge room called the Change House, where all of the contractor craft meet, eat and clock out for the day.

There are rows of picnic tables where the men kept their lunch boxes, etc. Off to the side were the general foremen's offices. Our electrical craft called this office the Woodshed and was occupied by my current General Foreman, "JAY" at that time. If you wanted to make money, Jay was the man. He always stood up for his employees and never would let a prospective job slip through his fingers. When egotistical craft supervisors tried to direct Jay's men, Jay would say, "There's a chain of command here, if you want my men to do something, you go through me!"

Once, a supervisor ignored Jay and attempted to give one of Jay's foremen direction. When the foreman told him to see Jay, the irate supervisor went to his supervisor to have the foreman fired. I happened to be in the office at the time and watched as Jay got in this guy's face. The supervisor demanded to his boss that both Jay and his foreman be fired. About ten minutes later, the oversight manager fired the supervisor.

This was the job climate I worked in.

Very strict and to the point—after all, it was a dangerous place to work with no margin for error.

The Woodshed

The Woodshed was no place to be. You always tried to avoid a trip there. And as long as you avoided the drama and did your job, you could avoid the Woodshed and getting on Jay's bad side.

Not saying a word to anyone about the owl incident, I quietly and nervously watched the clock tick down to quitting time. With one minute to go, it seemed I had dodged a bullet. Just then, the Woodshed door opened, Jay called me over, and said "I can't help you; you're wanted in the War Room now!"

I replied, "Now? It's quitting time."

Jay said, "Now. You'll get paid overtime to pack your things up."

With a lump in my throat, I made my way through the evening fog toward the administration building.

As I turned the corner, I saw a crowd gathered in the hallway, and I could hear a meeting going on in the conference room. There must have been a hundred people there.

Out of the room popped the containment coordinator with a huge grin on this face. Not trusting him, I was sure I was fired.

"Franny, come in," he said.

My heart was beating out of my chest as I entered the room. All of a sudden, I received a standing ovation. I was confused. Then the plant manager said that because of me, an owl was saved and we could get the outage back on schedule.

I received a commendation letter, a flashlight, two $50 American Express certificates.

I was in shock.

The Nuclear Engineering Department named a star after me and sponsored a great horned owl in my name at the zoo. The local paper followed up the next day with a story about how the owl left the containment building.

The article never mentioned my name, but the plant spokesman said, "A creative worker managed to get the owl out unharmed!"

Two months later, Rising Sun Energy aired commercials on prime-time television showing one of their in-house utility crew members climbing up a tower to put an osprey hatchling in a nest. My fellow workers joked that that should have been me.

Not My Close Call

When I worked as a teen during the construction phase of Triumph No. 1, a young engineer named Habib recently had arrived from a project in the Middle East. Habib played an integral part in the design and construction of this massive undertaking.

From time to time, Habib's path would cross mine and we would exchange pleasantries, however, I had not been assigned to any of his projects. Years later, our paths crossed when I was working in Temporary Power and Light support for one of Habib's projects.

During preventive maintenance testing of steam generators at other nuclear stations, small holes and pitting were found within the generators' tubes. If any of these generators failed, it potentially could force the control room operators to implement a hot shutdown of the reactor, which is never a good thing since it removes the unit from producing electricity to the national wide distribution grid. This set off alarm bells that eventually made their way to the Nuclear Regulatory Commission in Washington, DC. The NRC mandated every pressurized water reactor plant in the nation had to undergo comprehensive testing of the steam generator tubes. If the test results were outside of the engineering parameters, mitigation would be needed to ensure the safe operation of the generators and the plant. Although corrections had been made at plants throughout Europe and Asia, this would be a first for the U.S. nuclear plants.

Mitigation consisted of two options:

1. Replace the faulty generators with ones created for plants that had not gone online nor would due to the construction moratorium.

2. Try an unproven method of re-lining the slightly blemished tubes, while blocking off any tubes that were severely pitted.

Rising Sun Energy decided that the cost of this unproven method was not a viable option. The company's engineers found four steam generators at an unfinished nuclear plant in another state that had never been put in service due to the moratorium. If the test results of the current generators didn't meet safety and performance parameters, the massive job of removing the highly radioactive contaminated steam generators would be undertaken and they would be shipped offsite, buried, and replaced with the unused generators.

In preparation for the testing by an outside contractor from France, my co-workers and I supported this group by installing remote-controlled cameras, cables, electrical, and lighting support. Since most of the replacement generators had been completed outside of the United States this massive, first-time project became the "Super Bowl" of U.S. nuclear plants. Trade journals carried the stories and advertisers took full advantage of this replacement evolution.

Outside the reactor building was a trailer with several monitors tracking cameras positioned all over the plant. Inside the plant cafeteria was a large-screen TV monitor. Upper management, visitors, VIPs and plant personnel could view whatever activities the plant manager requested of the controller in the trailer. The trailer was attached to a larger one where the workers would change and take their breaks.

The ball breaking carried out between workers while changing clothes or on breaks could be pretty harsh, which was typical among some of the construction crews, however, these workers were battle-hardened and had thick skin. One day, the CEO from the testing contractor flew in from France with his translator for a meeting with the Chief Nuclear Officer (CNO) and staff of Rising Sun Energy's corporate offices. After a tour of the reactor building, the two men went into the trailer to change at the same time that some workers were there on their coffee break.

Boy, was that a mistake. The two Frenchmen had their backs to the workers and faced the lockers while they disrobed and changed back into their suits. The sight was a shock to the smart - ass construction workers. The Frenchmen were wearing thongs—flowery hiney floss. A pipe-fitter foreman said, "Hey, Frenchie, nice panties."

The French CEO asked the translator what the foreman had said, and the translator told him. The two then stormed out of the trailer. Since this foreman was a critical employee, I doubt he was reprimanded.

The next day, shortly before lunch, I walked past the monitor room to see one of my Rad Pro Tech friends in charge of controlling the cameras.

"Hey Scott, how are you doing?" I asked.

He replied, "Franny, thank god you're here. I have to take a shit really bad. I'll be lucky if I get to the bathroom in time. Could you please watch these cameras for a couple of minutes until I get back?"

"Sure, Dude, go take care of business," I said.

He replied, "Cool, I owe you big time. Thanks!"

His mistake was leaving me in charge. My intentions were never to cause mischief, it just dropped in my lap. As I scanned each monitor, I noticed that most showed nothing since it was close to lunch, and the only people working were on overtime. I saw some activity on one of the cameras. A man suited up in a high radiation area was on a platform under one of the two steam generator hatches. This platform was like a boxing ring with a camera situated in each corner. I knew it well since another electrician and I installed them. The man obviously was supporting workers inside the hatch. The camera was facing him head-on. He was on his knees vigorously filing something. Just then I panned the camera around to the other corner to find another guy sitting on a toolbox dozing off and waking up just as he would nod off.

Hmm. What if...I thought!

Since these guys were diagonally across from each other, approximately eight feet, what if I turned on the camera in back of the guy who was on his knees filing? So, I turned that camera on and because of the angle of the camera, the distance was lost in the picture. It looked like the guy nodding off was receiving oral gratification from the guy filing. Now all you saw was the back of the guy on his knees going up and down, and the other guy leaning back and waking up surprised. I never laughed so hard in my life. This happened to get the attention of my co-workers heading to the trailer to change for lunch.

"Jesus, Mary, and Joseph!" one of the pipe fitters said.

A carpenter said, "My God, is he really doing that?"

One of the laborers said, "He should get fired for having sex in a contaminated area. Save that shit for home."

Just then one of the electricians said "Dude, send that picture to the cafeteria large screen. They're having a huge meeting with VIPs right now."

I obliged and hit the keyboard. Our friendly rad pro tech, Scott, was making his way through the twenty or so men crowded around the doorway.

"Thanks, Franny. What in the hell are they all laughing about?" Scott asked.

I replied, "Look at the monitor."

Scott, half laughing, yelled, "Holy shit!!"

Just then a red phone on his desk began to ring. Scott answered, "Hello? What?"

With the phone in his hand, he said to me, "Dude, what in the fuck did you do?? Hello, no sir, not you! I was talking to…I'm sorry, sir, I'll move it immediately."

"Franny, I'm going to kill you after I get fired. That was the plant manager, and he is pissed. Are those guys really doing that?"

Just as I was leaving, I could hear the phone ring again and Scott tell the person on the phone, "Hello, Scott Ramsay, employee number RP-5176…"

It took me about twenty minutes to recover from my stomach cramps from laughing so hard. I never found out what happened to Scott after that incident. I never saw him again, but I overheard other Rad Pro workers remark that Scott got a job on the West Coast as a surfing instructor.

Oh well, shit happens.

ORAM RED

"Those who don't know history
are doomed to repeat it."

–Edmund Burke

Introduction

"Post September 11, 2001"

The Nuclear Regulatory Commission determined that the security systems at the nation's nuclear power facilities were gravely inadequate and could pose serious security issues if not corrected. To remedy this, contractors were hired by the nuclear utility providers to beef up their security systems with funding provided by the federal government.

Once security engineering reviews were performed, upgrades were made to perimeter fencing, alarm systems, and video surveillance using state of the art technology. Vital area entrance and main gate upgrades were also completed. Security personnel were eliminated as a result of the modernization of the surveillance systems. Unfortunately, new technology has its drawbacks, in this case employee layoffs. Additional guard towers and video surveillance were added to the river area facilities and the service water facility buildings.

There is a main Security Center, which includes security guards, bomb detectors (aka sniffers), X-ray conveyor and hand/card reader turnstiles, that all personnel pass through when entering the plant. The Security Center also contains a sally port entrance where incoming vehicles, mostly trucks and vendors are searched for contraband, weapons, bombs, etc.

When properly cleared, an armed escort accompanies visitors through the facility for deliveries or pickups.

In a secured bunker below the Security Center is the main communications center as well as an armory, changing facility, gym, showers, snack room, and lounge for the guards. Picking up guard escorts, visitor badges, and detentions also occur in this facility. No one would ever dream this building would become ground zero for a disaster that had the potential of killing thousands.

A story that would be unknown forever, except by the people involved in it. The ultimate cover-up.

TIME TO HEAD TO WORK

t was a crisp fall morning as I drove down the long access road in the dark. The smell of oysters and Pluff mud exposed at low tide permeated the air. I loved the early morning hours in the fall and especially seeing the meteors that would streak across the black velvet sky.

As I drove, I could see the reactor building as well as the blinking aviation strobes atop Triumph 1's imposing five-hundred-eighty-foot concrete cooling tower peeking through a light fog in the distance.

It is outage time, when the nuclear reactor and associated equipment are maintained and refueled. It was the same routine for me every eighteen months during the refueling process. I would find my peace each morning after I grabbing a buttered roll, newspaper, pack of cookies, and coffee with lots and lots of sugar from Larry's Country Store.

I loved to sample the fresh-baked pastries that Larry's received from the local bakery. However, before smoking was banned, the young girl who worked the counter had returned to college and was replaced with her chain-smoking elderly aunt. It was common to see the woman lean over the uncovered pastries and take money from customers as a cigarette dangled from her lips while the ashes decorated the icing on these once-delicious pastries.

What the hell, I didn't need the extra calories anyway, and stuck with the prepackaged peanut butter cookies.

As I would continue my drive to work, I was reduced to listening to the boring BBC News on National Public Radio on the terrestrial FM band since my pay satellite radio station had deleted my favorite morning channel from their lineup, replacing it with the NASCAR Radio Channel. The missed Book Radio.

I never thought I would get into that sort of genre, but after getting addicted to "The Harry Nile Mystery Series," as well as the short stories, I was hooked. Sadly, it had been eliminated from the daily lineup.

After successfully passing through the security checkpoint on the main access road, the challenge began—the daily fight for a close parking space. I could understand the frustration felt by the permanent in-house workers having to compete for parking with hundreds of contract workers during the refuel outages.

This daily game of musical cars plays out during every refueling outage. If you were smart you would time your arrival to coincide with the changing shift. If you were really smart you would pick a space and time when you knew a familiar car would depart. I would rather get there 45 minutes early to get a closer space than have to walk a half-mile in the rain, snow, sleet, or occasional hail.

Getting there early also gave me time to enjoy my coffee, snacks, and newspaper, even if it meant I would be sitting in my car for a bit. Besides, the winds and rain coming off the Squankum River were notoriously brutal in the fall and winter.

As I walked to my office, I glanced up at Triumph's cooling tower aviation strobes. Every day I could hear the crackling of the 500 KV lines in the switchyard, which on this particular day, was covered in a dense fog.

Before 9/11, you would have been able to park outside the switchyard fencing. However, after the terrorist attacks, the parking area was moved farther to reduce sabotage potential. On a foggy, damp morning you could feel the static electricity on the metal parts of your vehicle. Sometimes, the hair would even stand straight up on your arms.

As I stepped into the engineering building, I could smell the coffee brewing in the cafeteria. As always, I never used the elevator, but took the long stairs to my floor. I made my way to my office located in a bombproof former vault that once stored the plant's print library along with sensitive documents.

Now that everything was digitized there was no need for physical document storage. This left a new and convenient way to hide away contractor supervisors. Why not keep them in the vault?

As an outside contract electrical supervisor, it could have been worse. I could have been working out of a broom closet or a basement.

Walking around the corner of the office cubicles I saw the backside of everyone's favorite custodian—Bob—as he stood halfway in his closet. Within the building, he was endearingly known as "Plumb Bob."

Plumb Bob was a seventy-two-year-old Navy veteran who had survived the Pearl Harbor attack on December 7, 1941—"a date which will live in infamy."

Plumb Bob was a true patriot and would never hold back a memory or story if given the opportunity to tell someone. It had been years since Clara, the love of his life, died from lung cancer. Now, he spent most of his off time with his old American bull terrier, Meatball. He loved fishing and telling lies to the other old vets at the local VFW hall. Most of the ladies were charmed by Plumb Bob. As I got closer, I heard him humming an old 1950s tune "Since I Met You Baby" by Ivory Joe Williams.

With a smile, I said, "Good Morning Bob, now I'll be singing that stupid song all day!"

Plumb Bob would entertain himself by humming a popular catchy song or commercial jingle as people passed by. You could hear him giggle as he heard people throughout the day humming or whistling his goofy song du jour.

This game he played had its risks. One day a tall, buxom brunette contractor clerk from Texas grabbed him by his khaki shirt, looked down at him, and said in a soft but firm voice, "If I hear you hum another stupid song as you pass by my desk, I will beat the living shit out of you, do you understand me?"

An embarrassed, red-faced Plumb Bob looked around and said to me, "You know Franny, I really get the feeling that she likes me, this could be true love."

I replied, "Bob, you might be right. There is a fine line between love and hate!" I sighed.

Heading to the vault I could hear giggling and Alphonse Moroni's voice. Alphonse was a tall, handsome, laid-back graduate of the University of Pennsylvania's engineering department. He was the supervisor of our motorized operated valve testing team. He also was a character with a great sense of humor and a good problem solver who just wanted to enjoy life to the fullest—and did.

It seemed that Penny, the sweet, mid-twenties custodian from the third floor, had a crush on Alphonse and would frequently hide out in our vault.

And why not? The six-foot-two Alphonse could have been a GQ model. He had a great, happy-go-lucky outlook

on life and spoke with a thick Italian accent often mispronouncing words. I liked to believe he did this on purpose
to get a rise out of people. He came in each morning with
a handful of lottery scratch-off tickets but never forgot to
save one for "third-floor Penny."

As I was getting ready to walk into the vault, I heard
Alphonse say to Penny, "Dida you win Penny? Ifa you did,
you cana quit youra farkin job anda leavea sum of a batchen
broom behind!"

He then turned to me and said, "How's a trick's, Franny?"

It was early that morning when we logged into our com-
puters. This was done in the War Room where all the senior
management, engineers, radiological protection (Rad Pro)
supervisors, planners, and maintenance staff gathered to
schedule, plan, and run the outages. Each day there was a
hands-on turnover between the night and day shifts. Updates
and critical job information were transferred between both
shifts at these important mandatory turnovers.

The daily morning plant status would not be put into the
computer system until this briefing was completed. Techni-
cally, we were prohibited to go into the field until we knew
what the current status was. Part of that status was knowing
the ORAM color—the Operational Risk Assessment and
Management status of the plant.

Each level was assigned one of four colors, signifying
safe to most critical:

Green: safe condition

Yellow: possible redundant systems in maintenance

Orange: unexpected safe shutdown or cooling issues

Red: critical system problems that must be corrected within 15 minutes or the plant manager must notify the NRC of a safety-related problem.

Major fines could be assessed in the last case.

A possible site emergency might be declared depending on the severity of the issue/issues.

While we waited for the status update, we would watch our favorite clips from the movie "Johnny Dangerously" on YouTube. This was where Alphonse picked up his annoying habit of purposely mispronouncing certain words. Watching these clips broke up the monotony and kept us in stitches throughout the day. Alphonse loved to mimic the main character in the movie since they both shared the same Italian accent. Alphonse had informed me that morning that we would have to suit up and head to a job in the RCA (radioactive controlled area) to see whether a step needed to be written in the work order to erect a scaffold that would reach the height of the MOV our crew had orders to work on.

We had contacted the carpenter's supervisor and instructed him to meet us in the protected clothing dress out area at 10 a.m. sharp.

Finally, after a cup of coffee and running through our updated plant status, we made our way to the Rad Pro office to receive our briefing.

Then we grabbed our electronic dosimeters and electronically signed into Rad Pro's computer monitoring system.

Clad in scrubs, we made our way to the dress out area. I remember when I was younger and dumber, hearing my old electrical general foreman Jay and other old-timers talk about the "good ole days" of going to the dress out area in underwear with the women alongside them in nothing but bras and panties.

I also remember the old-timers saying that whoever hired the women should have been complimented since they were "smoking hot."

As we approached the dress out area, we heard many voices. It seemed as though the laundry truck had been delayed and many people were backed up and waiting on fresh protective clothing. There was the typical idle chat between disciplines, contractor and in-house maintenance personnel.

The carpentry supervisor brought three union laborers with him on the walk down. The laborers would move the scaffolding and assist the carpenters as they assembled them.

We decontaminated, bagged and dose-rated electrical cords, and loaded the bags in specially designated sea van containers located at the reactor hatch. These sea van cargo trailers normally are transported by truck and loaded onto container vessels. However, these particular sea vans would be stored in a radioactive contamination area in the yard until the next refuel outage. This brought back fond memories of a time when our job was interrupted by a polar crane pick. This was a large crane located on railroad like tracks in the containment building. It was used to lift heavy components and could travel 360 degrees on the track. When this crane made a pick, you didn't want to be under or around the moving load. In this case, our sea van was directly under the pick, so we were moved to wait in a low-dose radiation area until the pick had been completed.

While we were in an "idle state," we would talk about cars, girls, food, and music—every guy's favorite subjects. I remember a funny conversation in this instance while waiting for the polar crane to lower the reactor head to the containment building floor.

The guys were talking about how they wished their girls would shave their lower regions. This had been considered a fetish at the time, and most men, if lucky enough to experience it, considered it a treat. All of the guys agreed that their better halves would say "absolutely not!" if asked to "shave it all off."

Their foreman shook his head at the stupidity of the conversation, but still managed to smile and laugh. Me, being the smart ass I was, could not miss this chance to have a little fun. Age-wise, I had a good seven years on the boys. One of the boys asked me whether my girl shaved down there?

With a surprised look on my face, I replied, "Just because I'm older doesn't mean I'm dead yet, of course she does!"

He said, "How did you get her to agree to your request?"

With a straight face, I replied, "With women, you need to use psychology. If you can get them to relate to something they love, you'll eventually get your way."

One of the guys asked, "How so?"

I replied, "Ask your better halves to describe their ultimate dream meal."

One guy said, "I know she'll say filet mignon with sauteed portobello mushrooms and a twice-baked loaded potato with lots of creamy butter and sour cream."

I then told him to tell her, "Suppose you were told that tomorrow night we are going to Ruth's Chris Steak House. We'll spare no expense to get that steak you love so much."

Then I said, "Now the whole next day she will be dreaming of that night. She can almost taste that tender and juicy piece of heaven. Her mouth is watering as the waiter passes by the both of you with other people's orders. You both have another glass of wine. Just then the waiter arrives as she takes in the seductive aroma."

At this point, I almost lost my composure as these guys were hypnotized by my enticing story. They were licking their lips and were focused on my every word. Since lunch-time was near, all of them were hungry. One of the guys said, "What does he say next? What does he say next?"

I said, "Now you tell her the waiter places that juicy, sizzling platter in front of her. She takes in that heavenly aroma, slices a piece of meat, and hoists it to her lips just to notice a large black pubic hair on her steak." They all agreed that her response would be "GROSS!"

One of the guys commented, "My wife would prob-ably vomit!"

I said, "Now you tell her…how do you think I feel when I get hair in my dish?"

Ah, the memories of past, stupid conversations.

Now, back to the future, our mini stand-down was over. I moved on to check the progress of the test team I had been supervising. They had been working on one of the highly radioactive containment pressurizer valves.

The next morning Alphonse and I had been informed by our counterparts on the night shift that the valves' wiring was so degraded due to radiation, heat, and the harsh envi-ronment, that it had to be completely rewired and would take a day just to have the parts flown in.

As we left this "hot turnover," we walked through Engi-neers Alley. As we passed the new hires, kids fresh out of college, we both got a killer glare from Youseff and his friend and fellow engineer Sunni. Youseff and Sunni both had gotten their jobs courtesy of Youseff's father, Habib. Habib and his wife, Fatima, had left the Middle East in the late 1970s to take a job with Rising Sun Energy Corporation's Triumph nuclear project.

When the facility was completed, it had the potential be the second largest nuclear facility in the United States. Although it had only one reactor in service, it had permission to build four additional ones. Habib was well respected by his colleagues and was the senior design engineer for Rising Sun.

After several years in the U.S., Habib and Fatima had two children—a daughter, Yasmine, and her younger brother, Youssef. They were two years apart in age.

Yasmine had been studying medicine at the local university while Youssef recently had graduated college with a degree in nuclear engineering.

Habib had managed to get Youssef and his former dorm mate and best friend, Sunni, entry-level engineering jobs with Rising Sun.

I said to Alphonse, "Did you catch those evil glares?"

Alfonse replied, "Yeah I sawa that too. Maybe theya havin a bad day or something."

As we turned the corner, Plumb Bob happened to be coming out of his custodial closet and heard me tell Alphonse, "If their eyes were laser's, we'd be on fire by now!"

As Alphonse laughed, Plumb Bob said, "I bet I know who you're talking about."

Alphonse said, "Okaya, Bob, who?"

Bob replied, "Those two young feller engineers. One of them is Habib's kid.

"Habib is a great guy. You should hear the way his son talks to him. It's a damn shame. Especially after Habib got those two ungrateful sons of bitches their jobs here. Surprised you two never heard 'em."

"Coma to think of it...I heard a commotion dee other day outside a da vault. When I peakeda my head out dey hada just clammed up and were a walking back to their desks," Alphonse said.

After work Alphonse and I met at the Well Tavern. This was the same place Bobby O'Donnell and I would pick up our daily six-pack on the commute home while carpooling during the construction phase of the Triumph Project years before. The Well was a post-World War II beer and shot joint located five miles from the plant's access road. It's a local hangout frequented by plant and outage workers after their shifts and is well-known for great early-morning breakfast specials and $5 Well burgers on Wednesdays.

No beer on taps here, just bottles, pool tables and segregated entrances and bathrooms left over from the 1950s. The place has been owned the whole time by Maggie and Jake McBride. This day had been nothing out of the ordinary. The place was packed with the usual regulars—nuclear security, in-house maintenance and supervision, out of town Rad Pro techs, and other craft.

We squeezed in a table occupied by Doreen, Lynn, and Joe, the popular in-house maintenance chief.

Doreen and Lynn were the best of friends. Doreen was a beautiful brunette who wouldn't take shit from anyone but somehow maintained a feminine softness. Lynn could have been a California beach girl. Golden brown tan, blonde hair, and freckles. She had been Doreen's best friend and supervisor.

A lieutenant in nuclear security, Lynn was a born-again Christian who found inner peace by sailing around the country with her husband, and former navy nuclear sub operator, and their little dog, Scarlett. Lynn said to

Doreen: "We have a force-on-force drill tomorrow due to an upgraded security threat level from the NRC in Washington. We shouldn't be out too late."

"Franny can tell youa where dat threat is," Alphonse joked.

Maintenance chief Joe said, "I'll bet I know who you're talking about. Habib's kid and his friend, Sunni."

Just then, Doreen said, "I've seen them in the cafeteria, and they give me the creeps!"

"I don't know who you're talking about, but he can't be too bad if he's Habib's kid," Lynn said.

Alphonse said, "Plumb Bob saida Habib and his kid Youssef constantly argue in da hall."

Doreen said, "I love Habib, he's so nice."

With that, Lynn gestured and said, "We gotta go, take care all."

I told Alphonse I was pulling the pin and he left too.

The next morning, we were informed that the pressurizer valve was ready to be rewired since all the parts had arrived early that morning. After our morning brief I sent the crew into the field to get their daily radiation briefing and to suit up. After a while Alphonse and I headed up to Rad Pro to get our briefing, suit up and then check up on our crews. Rad Pro had another check-in desk at 130-foot elevation in containment. Each floor is described by its actual elevation above sea level. Whenever we entered the containment structure, we always had to check in with the Rad Pro technician on 130-foot elevation for the latest radiological conditions.

Wouldn't you know it, all the crews had been standing down in the low-dose waiting area due to a polar crane pick. This time the crews had to wait in a safe area while the polar crane moved huge parts of equipment that they recently disassembled from one of the containment fan coil units.

I walked over to my favorite group of laborers. When they saw me approach, they were grinning from ear to ear. I had forgotten about the previous steak conversation, but they hadn't. One of the crew kept saying, "You da man! You da man! The beers on us the next time you're at the Well."

I asked, "Why? What did I do?"

"Remember our conversation about the steak story? Well, we all went home that night and told our girls exactly what you told us to say," one of the guys said.

"And, am I in trouble now?" I said.

One of the guys said the next day when he got home, he was called into the kitchen to hear his wife tell him she had a big surprise for him. He was thinking it might be a favorite meal she cooked. She said, "Close your eyes!" Then said, "Okay...look," as she pulled down her tight jeans revealing a sexy, silky pair of boy short panties.

Then she said, "Ready?"

She pulled down those silky panties revealing nothing but pink rose petals with nothing surrounding them at all, not even a stray hair.

The other guys shared similar stories. I must say for being the "hero of the day," I still haven't tasted that free beer I was promised.

While the outage work packages were quickly being completed, some of the less critical orders were being pushed to the next outage for budget reasons. The department heads had been desperate for their bonuses and were pushing hard to close these windows and get the plant back online and synced to the grid.

The test teams were finishing up their work packages, mostly performing post maintenance testing, as required, before turning those MOVs back to operations.

One testing supervisor, Greg Wallace, was a regular member of the MOV team. Greg was a Marine veteran, funny country boy, physical fitness nut, and an expert in NASCAR.

This guy loved to work out and it showed. Despite his Marine Corps firmness, Greg had a great sense of humor and just like a Marine, he always had your 6. And if need be... he'd give you the shirt off his back.

Greg, in his turnover to Alphonse and me said, "Most of the fuel movements had been completed last night, and I'm so glad. Soon I will be on my lake spending time with my girl GiGi."

Poor Greg had been stuck in his hotel room that past weekend.

Since it had been Thanksgiving weekend, the plant made these guys (none of them local), take the holiday off because they didn't want to pay overtime.

Many of these workers could not make it home and back in such a short time, so they spent their extra day off either in their motel rooms or eating their Thanksgiving dinner at one of the local greasy spoons.

Unlike the other workers, Greg was happy with this particular outage. His beautiful body-building partner/girlfriend had driven all the way from North Carolina to surprise him with a mobile Thanksgiving dinner with all the trimmings complete with pumpkin pie and fresh flowers. What a gal. Our tough Marine was beside himself with appreciation.

Alphonse had a good time with his two little girls and in-laws at his place.

Me? I was pleasantly surprised to learn my flight attendant girlfriend—Fly Girl—had bid to have Thanksgiving off, which as a flight attendant was nearly impossible, and she succeeded in getting the holiday off.

We enjoyed a home-cooked meal and a relaxing, quiet night at her farmette with her huge, cuddly cat Tiger. What a treat and surprise!

But I was back to the grind the next day. While getting a cup of coffee, I ran into Habib in the hallway.

"Hey Habib, 'How was your day off?'"

With a distressed look on his face, he said, "I wished I had worked the holiday."

I said, "Your daughter is home from school, Fatima is an incredible cook, and you have your working partner and son, Youssef. What more can you want?"

He said, "Franny, these kids today are different. It's almost as if they are possessed!"

I said, "Possessed? It's probably growing pains."

Habib responded, "At 25?"

I naturally assumed all didn't go well at his family dinner with Youssef. I asked him how Yasmine was making out in medical school. He said, "She's always doing great in her schoolwork, but she takes a lot of heat from her Middle Eastern classmates for being too American. They constantly chastise her for hanging around with the American girls. They tell her she's a traitor to Islam."

I told Habib it must be very stressful for Yasmine, and asked him how she responds to the bullying.

He said proudly with tears in his eyes, "She tells them she *is* an American."

Just then, Youssef turned the corner to find me talking to his father.

I said, "Hey, Youssef how are you?"

He looked at me with an evil glare and turned to his father and said, "We need to talk!"

I wished Habib a good day and as they walked away, I could hear Youssef yelling something in Arabic at his father. Since I had no children, I thought to myself, at least he has kids to fight with. With time, I'm sure this will pass.

After lunch, Alphonse told me I received a phone call from the processing center. The center does security background checks on all personnel and visitors. They also train, test, and perform mental health evaluations on anyone requesting a security clearance to gain access to the protected areas of the plant. The processing center also provides the badges for plant access and computer-based training for the requalification of badged workers and other personnel.

I called back and told Alphonse I had just gotten popped for a random fitness for duty test. This was a drug and alcohol test in which you had no more than fifteen minutes to get to the testing area. There were two ways of getting popped. One was a "random" in which they pulled an employee's number randomly. The other being "for cause" in which you were either involved in an accident or a supervisor or co-worker thought you were acting aberrantly or under the influence.

I said to Alphonse, "This late in the day??" Alphonse said to me, " Whena wasa da lasta time you gota popped? Five a years ago?"

I replied, "About that."

He told me to, "Stopa you bitching, go doa you ting anda tell Littla Jean I saida hello!"

He also told me he had someone who had gotten popped three times for a random test last week.

"Random my ass," I said.

Little Jean is an administration clerk for the in-processing center psychiatrist. Little Jean was known and loved by everyone who worked in the plant. I had been friends with her for many years.

Most of the plant personnel passed by her desk at some time to visit the plant psychiatrist for one reason or another.

When I got to the medical department, I signed my name on the roster and read the sign stating: "No Eating, Drinking, Chewing Gum or Belching in the last 15 minutes."

Jan, the nurse popped out and said, "Mr. O'Dowd, long time no see."

I said, "Really? No belching?"

She said, "Don't start your crap with me smart ass. You know the routine.

"Empty your pockets, wash your hands, pee up to the line in the cup, and the rest goes in the toilet, don't flush, wash your hands. You've got five minutes."

After doing as I was told, I went to Jan's cubicle to finish the rest of the process.

"Okay, O'Dowd, initials on the samples, then blow into the machine until it beeps!"

"0.00, good. Now I'll see you in five more years."

I told her, "Not for me!"

She said, "Where the hell do you think you're going? A private resort island down south somewhere?"

Without her knowing I was close to retirement, I told her, "Yes!"

"Good luck with that" she said. "Now take your skateboard and get the hell out of my office."

"Oh, and Franny one more thing, have a nice day!"

On the way out of the medical office, I popped my head into the psychiatrist's office to find Little Jean busy on the phone.

I whispered, "Hey, Jean, how are you?"

She motioned me to wait.

I nodded okay.

When she got off the phone Little Jean said, "Hey, Franny, do you happen to know Habib's creepy son and his friend?"

She said she overheard two security supervisors mention there was a serious problem with them.

She told me some of the engineering department personnel overheard the two talking some crazy shit.

She said that she couldn't hear everything, but did catch, "Filthy American scum, and my father is a traitor and should be killed as an infidel!"

I replied, "Killed? Really?"

"Why don't they do something about it?"

She told me one of the security supervisors said to the other, "I'm not losing my career over a discrimination suit. Rising Sun will surely fire me If I mention it. Besides they can't be serious, it's just talk."

Little Jean then said to me, "This is scary, real scary and you and your team need to be careful out there. I've got a bad feeling about this! And you should also."

ALL QUIET FOR NOW

———

I t was near the end of the outage and Engineering Alley was quiet. Youssef and Sunni were MIA. Layoffs for the craft had been taking place on both shifts all week. The plant was beginning to look abandoned. Some of the steady workers as well as many in-house maintenance personnel were doing "nooner or sooners," a crude term we used to take off half-days while the herd was being thinned.

I ran into Timmy, aka WTF—as in, "what the fuck"—a phrase he used frequently. Timmy was a retired union electrician serving as post-retirement supervisor for construction activities outside the protected area.

He had been located in a remote trailer on the Possum Creek within the owner-controlled area of the plant property. Timmy told me he was hosting a trap shoot that night and invited Alphonse, Greg, and me. He told us even if we couldn't make it to the shoot, we should stop by the club lodge afterward for some cocktails. The club is a members-only, local rifle and pistol range. It features a spring-fed lake, great bass fishing, on-site skeet and trap range, as well as a campground and beautiful lodge with a full bar. I told him Alphonse and I could make it after the shoot, but muscle head Greg probably would be at the gym since he recently had been transferred back to the day shift.

Later, at the club lodge, Alphonse and I were sitting at the bar having a cold one when the doors crashed open behind us.

Timmy appeared and yelled, "Hoodlums! What the fuck??"

He ordered his usual Crown Royal and said to us, "What are you homo's up to?"

Alphonse replied, "Youa know, samea toilet, differenta seat."

Timmy said, "I gota you seat righta here!" as he pointed to his crotch.

Then Timmy said, "Bartender, another round for these hoodlums."

Timmy then asked, "What's the deal with Habib's kid and his friend?"

We asked him what he had heard. He said, "Upper management wants to wax both kids before something bad happens, but no one wants to be involved in a lawsuit."

I asked him, "What kind of bad things?"

He replied, "Apparently both these guys have been talking some radical shit."

I said to Timmy, "Remember what our former general foreman, Jay, would have said? Keep your nose out of it. Look at all the overtime you'd get if those bastards destroyed the place. We'd be here for years rebuilding it.'"

Timmy said, "You know, he's right!"

"Follow the money trail, there's a lot of milk in this cow!"

I told everyone I had to go.

"5:30 a.m. comes quick, and with my, luck I'll get popped again with another FFD."

In a very loud voice, Timmy said, "FFD? 1992 was your last one, wasn't it?"

I said, "Good night!"

The War Room was buzzing

The next morning did come early. At least that's what it seemed like. Most of the outage layoffs were complete. Each craft had been whittled down to skeleton core groups to close out any remaining work packages. Supervisors were cleaning up procedures and paperwork. Temporary power and light were demoing, leaving only a couple painters finishing up in the water boxes and their respective "hole watches."

Hole watch is a term used to describe a person who is trained and qualified to tend to personnel who are in confined spaces. The sole duty of the "hole watch" is to check the qualifications, monitor, and log in all personnel who enter a confined space, which usually has one entrance and one exit.

Rad Pro techs or HPs—Health Physics Techs—were busy taking down the heavy lead blankets that protect workers from the normally excessive doses of radiation that would be received from the high radiation system components. These lead blankets effectively reduce the radiation levels to a safer level for workers while allowing their job stay time to be lengthened. As systems were coming back online, operators could be seen out in the field manipulating switches, valves, and breakers.

For some reason, that day didn't have the typical "end of outage" feeling.

Something didn't seem quite right. I wanted to express these feelings to Alphonse or the millwright general foreman, but I knew they both would say I was being paranoid.

The foreman would reach in his drawer and give me a "hurt feelings report".

This is an official looking but totally bogus form handed out to anyone who whined. It was a form full of check-off boxes that asked questions like:

1) Where were you when your feelings got hurt?

2) Exact location where feelings got hurt.

3) Do you need a hug, etc.?

To avoid this embarrassing confrontation,

I intentionally kept my feelings to myself.

I spent most of the morning trying to pinpoint what had been making me feel this way, but to no avail.

Alphonse was out with the testers somewhere in the plant gathering missing calibrated test equipment to take back to the calibration lab.

I had developed quite a list of calibrated equipment in my name that was unaccounted for. Prior to and during each outage, supervisors signed out calibrated equipment in their names. It was a mad rush to get to the calibration lab to get the best equipment before other craft and test groups got to it first. All kinds of test equipment, torque wrenches, meters, safety harnesses, and wrenches could be signed out of the lab, but only if your name is on the list.

Most of the names on the list are in-house maintenance personnel, contract supervisors, and select craft personnel. Anyone who signed anything out was personally responsible for its return by the end of the outage or when its calibration date expired. The bad part was that the supervisors let their teams take this equipment out in the field. Other groups that were not able to get the good equipment, commonly "borrowed" other teams' tools when they were not looking or on a break. When your workers got laid off at the last minute and you had no idea where they left the tools, your name was put on the daily delinquent tool list in the daily report. You literally could spend days looking for this equipment, especially if it happened to be locked up in another craft's gang box—large, lockable tool boxes. The smallest piece of equipment could cost between several hundred to many thousands of dollars. This time I was out in the field on the hunt too.

As I walked around the auxiliary building, going from gang box to gang box like a butterfly going from buttercup to buttercup, I ran into a dear friend I worked with a couple of years back. Maria was a black-haired beauty born in Ecuador. She was a young and incredibly smart engineer normally assigned to the nuclear fuels department in Engineers Alley, however, due to staff cutbacks, upper management required all the engineers to take turns as craft oversight in the field.

"Hey, Maria, how have you been? Your turn in the pickle barrel I see."

Maria replied, "Yeah, Franny, I drew the short straw this time around. It's great to see you. Post-outage walk-downs I assume?"

I said, "Yes, I'm rescuing missing calibrated tools."

"That sucks!" she said.

"Yeah, I know, tell me about it."

She asked, "Have you thought where you're going to retire?"

I laughed and said, "I told Jan in medical I would be on a private island off the southern coast."

Maria laughed and said, "Anything is possible with you, Franny. Do you know Habib's son, Youseff, and his friend, Sunni? They work with us in Engineering Alley."

I said, "Yes, I hear they are speaking a lot of radical crap."

Maria said, "Not only that…no one has seen them since the day after Thanksgiving. They happen to have visitors coming in tomorrow from a plant overseas."

I said, "Japan?"

She said, "No, somewhere in the Middle East. They'll be coming in tomorrow on visitor badges. I hope these two come back tomorrow; I sure as hell don't want to babysit these two guys, especially since I don't speak Arabic!"

I told her it was time for me to get going. "Take care, Franny, she said. "I think I'll quit and move out west and become a doctor!"

Lunchtime arrived, and I caught Alphonse and Greg in the cafeteria. Greg had been moved to days with us since his night shift was laid off. Now he was cleaning up paperwork with us. Greg and Alphonse filled in the main supervisor position once held by Dan Rudderow. Dan, a Navy chief vet was a legend in the test world. It took two men to fill his position when he decided to call it quits. A great, but sometimes crabby southern gentleman, everyone loved Dan, from the secretaries to the senior valve engineer.

It was a major loss and sad day when he decided to retire. I heard rumors he is living the quiet life, hunting and fishing somewhere in Alabama or Arkansas with his beloved dog. Buck.

Lynn sat down with us for a quick bite. Except for a reflective drill vest, she was carrying her normal gear—an AR-15, gas mask on her leg, 12-gauge shotgun, and 9mm pistol.

Alphonse said, "Heya Robo Cop, howa you doing?"

Greg chimed in with, "Damn girl, you wearing enough?'

I asked her how the force and force drills were going.

She told us, "Two guys were taken to medical for bug bites (they're out), one got sliced up on the accordion wire (he's out), another was twirling his pistol like a cowboy and accidentally discharged it getting him fired (he's out). His friends now call him Barney Fife.

"So, to answer your question, not well. Any sign of your two buddies?" she asked.

I told her they have been out since the day after Thanksgiving.

All she said was, "Creepy, gotta run. Gotta protect you guys from the evil terrorists." We heard her laughing as she left.

Sometime later, we were in the vault finishing paperwork when Plumb Bob poked his head in and said, "You fellers working overtime?"

We all looked at the clock.

"Shit," Greg said. "I'm going to be late for the gym."

I told him I was on his tail. As I walked past Alphonse, I said, "You're going to get whistle bit!" Alphonse replied, "Youa guys go ahead, Ia wanna to finnisha up somadees fargain loose ends."

I said, no problem, I would be stopping at the Well to meet Little Jean and Fly Girl for a couple of cold ones. Greg told us he would be pumping iron and to tell the girls "Hey"

The Well was packed by the time I got there. As I scanned the bar, I saw Fly Girl and Little Jean sitting at a table laughing and giggling like a couple of school girls.

I said, "Can I join you or are you going to keep all this laughter to yourself?"

Little Jean said, "Sit your ass down!"

Just then Fly Girl said, "Get us a fresh round of PBRs first."

I obliged. By the time I got back, Doreen and Lynn had joined the girls. Oh well, back to the bar I went for a couple more beers. This time when I got back to the table, I heard them talking about Youssef and Sunni.

Fly Girl told everyone that all of the flight attendants she worked with were on a "heightened state of awareness."

She said the flight attendants were being tested almost every day by possible terrorist cells to see how they would react to different situations."

Little Jean asked, "How so?"

Fly Girl said, "For example, they will create a situation with other passengers over nothing at critical times, such as takeoffs and landings. They know we cannot leave our jump seats at that time."

Lynn asked how she knew this.

Fly Girl told them, "Really pissed off passengers never let up and then threaten our jobs, disparaging us until they leave the plane, sometimes requesting to talk to a supervisor. The bad guys create confusion and observe our reactions, or lack of, then stand down as if nothing has even happened."

Lynn said, "Did you read the paper yesterday? We, nuclear security, had to call the marine police in the past two days because each day a speedboat with a group of young men tried to see how close to the plant they could get.

"Two separate days and two different speedboats, both with young Middle Eastern men.

"They told the cops they didn't know where they were. The cops gave both boats warnings for not having enough safety gear on board."

I told Lynn, "That's crazy! They didn't even ask any questions?"

"None that we know of. You know they don't like doing paperwork. Our supervisor said she requested a Coast Guard gun boat to watch the plant but was told their resources were all tied up escorting tankers to port," she said.

It was getting late. Despite the serious chatter, we all had a great time laughing and chewing the fat. Once again, 5:30 a.m. comes quick, and we all left.

TRAFFIC JAM ON
THE ACCESS ROAD

The next morning, I turned the corner of the access road to see taillights for a quarter-mile. All the way up to Checkpoint Charlie, the first gate you come to on the access road before reaching the plant's parking lot. Being early that day paid off for me. By the time I got to the checkpoint, I saw a van on the side of the road with nuclear security and state trooper vehicles with their lights flashing. It looked as though they were interrogating the driver.

As I headed into Engineering Alley toward the vault, I heard a lot of talking and laughter. "How's a tricks, Franny?" Alphonse said. "Ua justa missed third floor Sally."

I said, "Yeah, what's up?"

Alphonse replied, "Shea said da nuclear security team stoppeda van thata tailgated a car througha da gate. There wasa six guys in da van, nada from disa country, noa I.Ds, nada, dey wera all a foreigners."

I said, "I saw the cops and the van."

The phone rang. The millwright foreman picked up the receiver and said, "Greg is stuck on the access road, but he is here on site."

I told him, "Tell that gay body-building Marine if he got here earlier, he wouldn't have this problem."

We all heard from the phone, "Kiss my ass you damned Yankee!"

We all burst out laughing.

FAST-MOVING POLITICIANS

That was a special day at the plant. Not only did Youseff have visitors coming in, (it was common for engineers to host engineers from other nuclear plants), but The Possum Post, the plant's daily newsletter, said the facility's spokesperson would be escorting a state senator and other politicians on a tour of the plant. They normally tried to schedule these public relations events at the end of an outage so the politicians did not get pinned into a corner by a smart-ass contractor asking embarrassing questions. This day the plant had hand-picked a group of "suck-ass workers" to say pre-scripted remarks to make the plant look good to the politicians and press.

This brought back funny memories from years ago when we were working on a security upgrade project. The Y2K project was the brainchild of governments and security software engineers from all around the world who were unsure of the consequences of computer systems' clocks hitting the year 2000. A retired carpenter had been contracted to make a large-scale model of the plant, which was to be nestled just outside of the bomb sniffers and past the X-ray machines. It was to be used to orient a Japanese delegation of nuclear plant operators to the plant's various buildings. They were here to learn our daily operating procedures.

The attention to detail in this model was excellent—nothing was left out. From the guard towers and the Squankum River, to the miniature armed security guards located at different positions throughout the facility. Unfortunately for plant management, the carpenter did not add a plexiglass cover on the model. This lack of detail presented an opportunity for various smart asses, like me, to have a bit of innocent fun. After reading about the visit, the next day I bought a couple of bags of little, plastic dinosaurs from the toy rack at Larry's Country Store. After arriving at the security center early, I carefully placed the dinosaurs in strategic locations throughout the plant model. I forgot about the 360-degree camera mounted in the middle of the main security center lobby. A few hours had passed when a couple of workers and I witnessed hysterical laughing, pointing, and giggling from six five-foot-tall Japanese visitors gathered around the model saying in accented English, "GODZILRA, GODZILRA!"

The look on the plant manager's face was hysterical. With his gray hair, his face was so red he resembled a Jersey tomato with snow on the top. He yelled at the plant spokesman, saying, "I demand you find out who altered this model and fire their asses now!"

I was laughing so hard I was getting cramps in my stomach. The next day I saw the retired carpenter. He told me it was unbelievable how much they paid him to build the model. He said the reason he had returned was to install a plexiglass cover and the idiots who hired him were paying him just as much to install the top as they paid him to build the original model.

About an hour later, two security guards approached me with serious looks on their faces. I was friends with both, but business is business, and these guys are professionals. When security is an issue, friendships go out the window.

"Mr. O'Dowd," one guard said to me.

"We have you on camera placing plastic dinosaurs in the model. That is a procedure violation and is considered altering plant equipment, which is a serious fire able offense,"

With a sinking feeling in my gut I said, "I guess I'm fired now?"

He then said, "No worries. All day long my guards were recorded on camera moving the dinosaurs from one spot to another."

With a sigh of relief, I still had my job, at least for now.

Getting back to the politicians, this day I was roaming all over the plant doing job status walk-downs. I saw the politicians come through in their custom twelve-seat golf cart. I ran into Doreen who was going from one post to another.

I said, "Hey, Doreen, where did the entourage go? I saw them come in and that was it."

She laughed and said, "What a joke, we escorted them in, they did a fast loop around the yard, and then some suck ass got their picture taken with the senator and, boom, they were gone!"

I replied, "Like the pizza place, 30 minutes or less? You mean they never got to see you guys running around in full gear with your weapons drawn?"

She said, "Lucky for that. We lost another guard to a cat attack, probably rabies, and another guard missed a rung on a ladder outside of the turbine building. Luckily, he only twisted an ankle. Maybe after shift, Lynn and I may catch up with you and the gang at the Well for a couple much needed cold ones. Lord knows we both can use a drink right now!"

As I was roaming the plant, I saw Youssef, Sunni and their two creepy-looking visitors arguing with a guard about why they couldn't gain entrance to the control room hallway. They had entered the hallway just outside the relay room. The control room hallway can be entered through a door in the relay room hallway, however to enter the room you need the senior nuclear shift supervisor to authorize a security clearance upgrade. Only with this authorization can security upgrade your access in their system. Even though Youseff and Sunni are engineers, the senior nuclear shift supervisor won't authorize access to the control room unless they have a specific task, such as a job walk-down, or other work requiring consultation with the supervisor.

The supervisor would know of any scheduled work and surely would have denied them access. Had the supervisor found out about their attempt to gain access to the control room hallway without proper authorization, red flags would have gone up. However, being a blatant security violation by procedure, the security guard never brought it up to his supervisor, and therefore, the senior night shift supervisor never found out about the attempted security breach. Once again, no one had the courage to blow the whistle on these guys for fear of having to pay a visit to Human Resources for an interview and possible suspension or job loss. Chalk up one for political correctness and zero for safety.

Outside the vault, laughter could be heard throughout the hallway. The boys were cracking jokes about how fast the politicians blew through the yard. Alphonse compared it to an old "M*A*S*H" episode when the unit prepared for an entire week for a visit from Gen. Douglas MacArthur only to have him buzz through the camp without stopping for even a minute. As his jeep passed by the shocked soldiers,

MacArthur proudly saluted cross-dressing Cpl. Klinger, gussied up like the Statue of Liberty with sparklers shooting from the torch in his raised hand.

I asked the guys if anyone saw the politicians in the field. Greg said, "Franny, what don't you get? They were in and out in less than a half-hour. They never got their fat asses out of the golf cart." The day shift millwright foreman said, "Between the guards and the imaginary terrorists, it's a miracle they even got out that quick!"

I then told them the story of Youseff and Sunni trying to sneak two visitors into the control room hallway by way of the relay room.

Just then, the night shift millwright foreman came in early for his hot turnover. The night shift millwrights didn't get laid off because in-house maintenance department needed their expertise and resources to close out some of their valve packages.

Anyway, the foreman is a laid-back local guy who never gets excited or goes off half-cocked.

It was very unusual to hear him say, "Something's not right about that whole situation." "My stepdaughter is friends with Habib's daughter, Yasmine. According to her, there was a big blowout between Habib and Youssef at their home during the Thanksgiving holiday. Yasmine told my stepdaughter that her brother, Youssef, hangs out with extremists and it is scaring his mother half to death."

We all agreed we should stay alert and maintain a state of situational awareness at all times.

DELIVERY DRIVERS HIJACKED

The next morning, I went for my regular morning fare at Larry's Country Store. The plant's delivery people parked their box trucks across the street as they waited for their coffee and morning goodies. It was always the same drivers making deliveries to the warehouse. Half of the warehouse is located outside the gate in what is called the clean area. The other half is located in the protected area inside the warehouse, where a huge room is divided by a wall and a set of closed bay doors that lead from the clean area, which has an armed guard 24/7, to the protected area.

No unauthorized personnel can enter through these doors without permission from the security supervisor. All goods delivered on the clean side must be inspected by quality assurance personnel for explosives and to meet their nuclear grade criteria before gaining entry authorization to the facility.

On this particular morning, we were unprepared for the events to unfold. According to witnesses, men dressed in nuclear security clothing hijacked by gunpoint the drivers of three delivery box trucks. Since off-site emergency drills were frequent in the county, the witnesses assumed it was a drill and didn't notify authorities. All three trucks passed through the access road security checkpoint with ease, and then backed up to the closed bay doors. With a wave from the warehouse forklift operator, all three doors opened, and a warehouse worker, as well as the forklift driver, watched in shock as the drivers and their fake guard escorts unlatched and opened the back of the three delivery trucks.

The phony guards quickly jumped out of the trucks, killing all three drivers, the warehouse security guard and a worker. With guns pointed at the forklift operator's head, he was forced to open the internal bay door using the dead guard's key. The fake guards quickly rushed to the other side, killing the forklift operator as they passed. They took control of the warehouse without a fight. The leader of the fake guards used one of the phones on the wall to call Youssef and inform him they were on-site and in position. All remaining warehouse personnel had their hands ty-rapped and mouths duct-taped by the attacking force. Then they were herded into a locked storage room in the back of the building to be guarded by one of the impostor guards.

The leader of the attacking force told his fake guards to keep them alive in case they needed pawns to negotiate with.

UNAWARE OF
ANY UNUSUAL EVENTS

L ike most plant personnel at the time, I had no knowledge of what was happening in the warehouse. As I passed through the security center, I saw Youssef and his two visitors waiting for their visitor badges. Passing them I thought, "If looks could kill, I'd be dead right now. These are not nice boys."

By the time I got to the vault, most of the remaining work had been completed and there was a relaxed feeling in the room.

The guys were talking about their next jobs. Both of the millwright general foremen were getting antsy. These two can't stand idle time. Alphonse and I went over our morning status update unaware of anything happening out of the ordinary. The millwrights laid off everyone except for their night shift foreman who was currently with us on day shift. Both millwright foremen left to go out in the field to collect the last safety gear on the delinquent list.

I called the Temporary Power & Light foreman and told him my group was finished testing, which gave the all clear to remove the remaining temporary power panels, known as trans panels in the turbine building.

As I crossed the hall to the copier room for a cup of coffee, I noticed Plumb Bob's door was closed. I thought,

"That's really weird. The only time Plumb Bob's custodial closet door is closed is when he leaves for the day. Any other time he can be heard humming tunes in there with the door wide open."

When I asked Alphonse where Plumb Bob was, he replied, "Maybe da olda guy a got fargain lucky. I a needa to find him."

I said, "Why, what's up?"

He said, "Some somoda beech lockadup da shitter door! I donna wanna hava to go a upstairs every a time I needa to take a fargain piss."

I told him it was open when I arrived early that morning, then asked if there was now a cleaning sign on the door.

Alphonse replied, "Noa cleaning sign!"

I told him that was weird.

"Hey, guys, anyone seen the creepies and their visitors?" I asked.

Greg told me he saw them getting visitor badges in the security center when he was coming in the gate.

By the time Youssef, Sunni, and their two guests got to their desk, Youssef answered the phone and said in Arabic, "Have all but a couple of men secure the warehouse and have the rest meet me at the engineering building's delivery bay door."

Investigators found these details by eventually replaying the recordings from the many closed circuit television video (CCTV) cameras. The Arabic language could be heard in all of the recordings.

No one paid attention to these men leaving the warehouse and heading toward the engineering building since they all wore nuclear security guard uniforms. We learned later that one of the men in the attacking force owned a business that did all of the dry cleaning of the guards' uniforms. And it was not uncommon for nuclear security to tour the plant with their newly hired guards.

Sunni took five of the phony guards with him to the security center. Youssef's visitors took six men and headed toward the turbine building. Youseff and a couple of men headed to the bathroom on our floor. When Youssef unlocked the bathroom door, the men went in, with Youssef trailing behind.

Habib saw Youssef go into the bathroom with the men. As Habib approached his son, Youssef pushed his father back into the hallway. Then, Youssef started to unlock the custodial closet with the confused Habib standing next to him. Habib said to Youssef, "What in Allah's name are you doing? Where's Plumb Bob? What are those men doing with weapons in the bathroom?"

Youssef opens the custodial closet door. A shocked Habib had terror in his eyes as he saw Plumb Bob sitting on the floor in a puddle of blood with his throat cut. Youssef pushed Habib in the closet as his father yelled, "You can't do this! It's foolish!"

Youssef placed his hand on Habib's mouth as he plunged a cold, steel blade deep into his father's chest. As the knife went in, he whispered to his father, "You will now die like the traitor you are."

Dead in his arms, Youssef shoved Habib deep into the closet and locked the door. Youssef headed back to the bathroom and gathered the men. Then they left for the relay room.

NO CALLBACK

found it odd that I hadn't received a phone call from the TP&L foreman to remove the trans panels they had installed for us. It wasn't like him not to call me back. I assumed he was busy, so I decided to take a stroll through the turbine building to see what equipment still remained.

Like the containment building, all of the floors in the turbine building are identified by their elevation at sea level.

As I got closer, I noticed a new sign that said, Hearing Protection Now Required!

Since the components had been rapidly coming online, the turbine building was now back to its normal deafening sound. Previously, the safety department had designated the area as a zone where no hearing protection was needed. With most of the components quickly getting back online, that designation was now history. As I walked on the steel grating of the turbine floor, I peered through the openings to get a view of the floor below, at the 88-foot elevation, hoping to possibly see TP&L electricians disconnecting cables.

I didn't see a soul and thought, "They laid off the whole TP&L crew? Can't be."

I decided to take the stairwell up to the next floor, 120-foot elevation, for a peek. On the 100-foot and 120-foot elevations, a majority of the pumps, valves, and other equipment are situated mostly on steel grating while the remaining parts of the floor are on concrete. As I popped open the door at the 120-foot elevation, the sound was deafening, even with ear plugs, the noise was twice as loud as the elevation below. I looked toward the mobile trans panel on the concrete floor that was supposed to have been removed. Cables had been strewn all around the trans panel, and there was as an electrical foreman's hard hat (identified by the stripe of yellow tape on it) and a pair of safety glasses. There was blood all over everything. I looked around, but there was no one in sight. I thought maybe while taking the cables down, the electrical foreman was injured, which is a rare, but possible scenario since everyone is well trained in safety and accident prevention.

TP&L electricians always work in pairs per plant procedure when disconnecting the huge 480-volt cables, but I didn't see anyone. I continued to walk on the grating toward the water boxes.

As I approached the railing, I noticed a confined space attendant (aka a hole watch) manning his post in front of one of the open hatches and holding a clipboard.

The hole watch's sole duty was to ensure that personnel entering the confined space are qualified and have been briefed on the conditions and stay times. They also log personnel, tools, and materials going in and out of that permitted confined space.

Hole watch attendants are never, under any circumstances, permitted to leave their posts when a worker is occupying the hole unless it is a life-or-death emergency. If a "person down" situation was to be encountered, they are supposed to contact site fire protection immediately. I asked the attendant who was working in the hole.

"Big Gary, the painter," he shouted.

I nodded to him as I walked away. As I rounded the corner, I thought I heard something that sounded like a gunshot. With noise this loud, your mind sometimes plays tricks on you and makes you think you hear things you really didn't.

I brushed it off as my imagination and continued to look around. No one there. As I headed back toward the water boxes, I noticed the hole watch was gone.

What the hell? Big Gary could not have gotten out of that hole in just two minutes. Impossible, I thought, and I walked over to the hatch the attendant had been watching. The attendant's clipboard was on the grating covered in blood.

I yelled into the hatch, "Anyone in there?"

Big Gary yelled back, "Yeah me! What in hell is going on out there? Where's Jimmy, my hole watch?"

I yelled back, "Gary, it's Franny. Get the fuck out of there now!"

Gary climbed out of the hole drenched in sweat. "Where's Jimmy? I'm gonna kill that kid!

"Why is the entrant list covered in blood?"

I told him we needed to go somewhere quiet to talk. We headed toward the elevator shaft room. I told Gary I had spoken to Jimmy not more than five minutes ago. I also told Gary that I was in the building checking to see if our equipment had been removed since I had not received a call back from the TP&L foreman.

I told him I found a TP&L foreman's hard hat and safety glasses on the floor with cables covered in blood.

Gary said, "Let's go to the break area and call someone to figure out what in the hell is going on around here. Besides, I could use a cold drink."

Just as I started to open the door, I quickly slammed it shut as two men in nuclear security guard uniforms ran by with their guns drawn.

Gary said, "Let me see," as he peered through the small glass window in the door. He then said, "Something's not right I know all the guards in this plant, and I've never seen any of those guys before."

Big Gary said, "The force-on-force drill" was over at least a day or so ago."

Just then we heard the pop, pop, pop of rifle fire. Gary took another look out of the little window and said, "They're not our security guards. We're being taken over by terrorists."

DASH TO HORROR

---

said, "Let's make a dash to the storage closet in front of the stairwell. There's a phone in there on the back wall. We can call security and figure out what in the hell is going on."

We looked around and made a dash for the doors to the large storage closet. As we popped inside, we closed the door behind us and locked the dead bolt. We then turned toward the back where the phone was located and a look of horror spread on our faces. Jimmy, Big Gary's hole watch, the two TP&L electricians, a fire watch and an in-house maintenance worker were all shot dead and stacked up like cordwood in the corner of the room under the phone whose cut cord was dangling above the bodies.

Our adrenaline kicked in, and we knew we had to act quickly.

I said to Big Gary, "We gotta get the hell out of here, we seem to be up shit creek without a paddle!"

We watched through the little windows in the double doors as five fake security guards took positions on the grating behind pumps and valves on the turbine deck floor. We would not make it more than twenty feet or so if we tried to make a run for it.

Big Gary said, "Fuck, what are we going to do? They may have taken over the whole plant!"

I told him I had an idea. All of those clowns had been hiding behind objects on the turbine floor grating. We counted five who we needed to get past to make it to the stairwell and out safely. The mobile electrical disconnect switch that was feeding our trans panel was five feet in front of us directly behind two stacked, extremely toxic hydrazine pallets. While disconnecting the trans panel, the electricians managed to get as far as taking the load end plug off of the 480-volt cord, which was coming from the mobile disconnect switch that was located on the concrete portion of the turbine deck floor. I noticed that the switch was still being fed from the 480-volt power tree.

It takes between 0.1 and 0.2 amps to kill a human. These mobile switches have 100-amp fuses in them. I told Big Gary I would crawl out on the floor and pinch the bare wires in between the steel grating. After I crawled back onto the safe concrete, I motioned to Gary to throw the switch to the on position. Bang! Smoke and fire everywhere! These pricks looked like they got caught up in a human bug zapper. Their clothes were on fire. As we ran toward the doors to the stairwell, all we could smell was the stench of burning flesh and hair. There was smoke everywhere.

SECURITY CENTER TAKEOVER

While the other men had taken over the security center, killing three guards, they also managed to get into the secured command center armored communications bunker by discreetly pointing a gun at a guard trying to gain entrance. There is a camera in the hallway outside of the heavy steel door. Once they were in the command center bunker, they killed that guard and two others who were at camera monitoring stations. They spared Lynn who was at her station. With a gun against Lynn's head, they commanded her to shut down the service water building cameras on the river. They told her if anyone called with questions to tell them it was only a drill. Back in the hallway, the fake security guards forced a security supervisor to unlock the door to the armory. Once they gained entrance, they shot and killed the supervisor.

During her rounds, Doreen saw two powerboats filled with men and guns on the river tying up their mooring lines to the service water building.

Another security guard impostor, located inside the fence on the plant side, opened the double razor-wire security fences to the river letting the men gain entrance. Doreen called Lynn on her radio. "Control, Lynn!"

Doreen said, "What in the hell is going on out here?"

Lynn replied, "Sharon do not engage. It's just a drill!"

Doreen got a horrible chill down her spine as she watched the progression of the armed men. She thought, "Why in the hell did she call me Sharon? She knew it was me. This is totally fucked up! Something really bad is happening."

Immediately her S.T.A.R (Stop, think, act, and review) training kicked in, along with her conditioned questioning. Doreen had taken her training seriously. She quickly dodged into one of the service water building hatches. Inside, she found a phone on a back wall near some electrical switch gear.

Just as she went for the phone, she felt a huge drop in pressure in her ears. This building, like most in the plant, are pressurized. Wherever you are in the room, when someone enters, you know it because you can feel the drop in pressure in your ears. The rooms in this building are also extremely noisy and you must wear earplugs or you will most certainly go deaf.

Knowing someone entered, she placed her rifle behind the switch gear and drew her 9 mm pistol as she took cover around the corner. A muzzle from a rifle came around the corner first. Doreen popped the rifle out of the gunman's hands. He knocked the pistol out of her hand. She quickly grabbed a fire extinguisher off the wall and hit him in the face. She then pulled the pin and sprayed him with carbon dioxide, dropping him to his knees. When she got back to the phone, she tried calling for assistance from anyone—the fire department, security, control room—but no one answered.

ACROSS THE PLANT

Meanwhile a couple of buildings away, not far from Doreen, more terror was taking place. In the auxiliary building just outside of the control room, Youseff and his two visitors once again tried to swipe in their access cards from the relay room hallway to gain entrance to the control room hallway. Knowing they would not get in, within three minutes a real guard showed up, just as before. The two men with Youssef quickly overpowered the guard and had him clear the door.

After using the real guard to gain entrance to the control room hallway, they killed him and grabbed his weapons while taking his access badge to gain entrance to the very busy control room. The senior nuclear shift supervisor barked at them, "What in the hell is going on here, and who in the hell are you guys?"

Youssef grabbed a pistol from one of his visitors and shot the supervisor dead.

"Listen up, everyone. We now own this control room, you will do exactly as I say, or you will die!" Youseff said.

Up above on the turbine deck, a couple of ironworkers, both Vietnam veterans were smoking cigarettes with their two apprentices. One of the apprentices was a former mixed martial arts fighter and the other a Marine force recon veteran of the second Gulf War.

These guys were neatly tucked in behind an elevator entrance on the top of the turbine deck 140-foot elevation, which also is the roof of the building. The elevator leads to the relay room, switch gear room and the control room. They were there to demobilize a crane that had been used for heavy picks during the outage and had an ideal spot to take a nice, long smoke break. From where they were, they had an unobscured view of most of the turbine deck. They also had a clear view of the Squankum River and the guard outpost at the edge of the turbine building. In addition to the guards' normal armament of an AR-15, 9 mm pistol, and gas mask, this particular outpost contained a .50-caliber Barrett's rifle in case of an assault approaching from the river. Fifteen minutes earlier, the guard who manned the river outpost called the security command center to report the two oncoming boats, however, he was reassured that they were only part of a drill.

Most of the turbine building components were back online. The noise on the turbine deck was deafening. Across the deck, about a hundred yards away, three fake guards emerged from an equipment elevator. Two of the men headed toward the regular elevator entrance where the ironworkers were hiding while the other fake guard walked toward the guard outpost on the edge of the building toward the river. A real guard came halfway out of the booth and yelled to the approaching fake guard, "What in the hell is going on? I can't get through to anyone on the radio or phone."

All three guard impostors aimed their rifles and shot the outpost guard. The fake guard made his way toward the real guard now squirming on the turbine deck and shot him three times with his pistol. After finishing off the guard, he then dragged his body into the booth. The horrified ironworkers could not believe what they had just witnessed. The two fake guards heading toward the elevator entrance did not see the ironworkers duck behind the structure. The ironworkers could hear the men talking in Arabic within the elevator structure. They were waiting for the elevator, however, there was only one problem. Workers used a trick to prevent their supervisors from checking up on them when they were in the smoking area behind the elevator structure entrance. They would prop the door open just a little bit. This building also was pressurized. If the door on the roof-top structure was kept ajar, the elevator doors would not open when it arrived on the roof at the 140-foot elevation. These bad guards did not realize this, so they waited and waited. As they were talking inside, the ex-Marine ironworker apprentice recognized the language the men were speaking and told the other guys that these men and others had taken over the plant. Since the bad guards were not going anywhere soon, the ironworkers devised a plan to incapacitate them. Three of the workers went to one side of the elevator structure door while the former Marine apprentice went to the other. All were armed with heavy spud wrenches.

"Crack," the ex-Marine smacked the door with his wrench and then ducked around the corner of the building. The two fake guards rushed out with their guns drawn. Using their spud wrenches, the three other ironworkers smacked the two fake guards on the back of their heads, dropping them to the deck. They grabbed their rifles and dragged their motionless bodies to their work tent around the corner. Removing items from their gang box, they duct-taped their mouths, wrapped their hands, and hogtied them to the railing while tossing them over the side of the turbine building railing about 140 feet in the air with the former MMA apprentice ironworker yelling, "You assholes fucked with the wrong group of union ironworkers!"

RELAY ROOM TROUBLE

———————

The relay room is a couple of floors below where the ironworkers were having their fun.

The relay room contained all of the plant's vital electrical controls and is one floor below the control room.

In the back of the relay room, high up in the cable trays, an electrical foreman and two other electricians were working on a design change package to label newly installed cables that had been pulled during the outage. Like many other rooms in these buildings, the relay room is pressurized. High above in the cable trays, they were quietly labeling cables unaware of the events taking place around them. On the floor below the electricians, there were two in-house instrument and calibration (INC) technicians working inside a control cabinet. A real security guard was making her rounds about the room. Sunni had ordered the two men inside the relay room to stand by just in case the equipment needed to be sabotaged. Being design engineers for the plant, Youssef and Sunni were familiar with the layout of the rooms, but they overlooked the type of fire suppression system there. Using a dead guard's access badge, they entered the room. The electricians could feel the pressure drop as they watched the two men approach the unsuspecting INC technicians. Pop, pop, pop, the stunned electricians watched helplessly as the fake guards shot the

INC techs. The real security guard, hearing the shots, ran around the corner only to be killed as well.

One fake guard took a position by one of the many pagers as another stood by a phone on the nearby wall. The fake guard got on the pager and in Arabic said, "Youssef, we are now in position."

The three electricians knew they were in serious trouble and needed to do something quick to make a getaway. Because the fire suppression was back online, each worker in the overhead was required to have an ELSA (emergency limited supply of air) pack with them at all times. Each ELSA pack had enough air to last about twenty-five minutes. Inside the ELSA pack pouch was a bag to be worn over the head with a hose connected to an oxygen tank. The idea was to give the wearer enough time to escape an area where a Cardox fire suppression system had been activated. Once activated, there would be a mint scent released into the area alerting properly trained workers to vacate the area within thirteen seconds.

The Cardox system is preferred in critical electrical areas because it displaces any oxygen, therefore, suppressing fires while not compromising the equipment with water or corrosive liquids.

The electrical foreman told both electricians someone would have to get to the fire alarm and activate it. All three donned their ELSA packs while one of the electricians quietly shimmied down the ladder and made her way over to the fire alarm. By the time she got there, all three electricians had turned on the oxygen valves on their ELSA packs. The other electrician yanked down the fire alarm handle. Just then, annunciator lights and sirens lit up the board in the control room.

Youssef screamed at an operator, "What's happening?"

The quick-thinking operator said, "It's a standard test of the fire suppression system." The operator then silenced the siren and lights on the annunciator board.

The three electricians in the relay room watched as both fake guards dropped to the floor while gasping for air. Within a minute, both were dead.

The three electricians exited and quickly escaped to the elevator entrance heading to the turbine deck roof where the ironworkers were hiding.

Having closed the elevator entrance door, the elevator made it to the top. Armed with the fake guards' rifles, the ironworkers waited to see who would emerge from the elevator entrance. As the three electricians exited, the ironworkers, poised to fire, recognized them and yelled, "Over here, quick!"

The electricians ran to the work tent where the ironworkers were. All of a sudden, the contractor Teamster seemed to appear from behind nowhere, startling everyone.

The electrical foreman asked, "What in the hell is going on around here?"

The ironworkers told the electricians, "It looks as though a terror cell has taken over the plant. They're wearing stolen guard uniforms."

An electrician asked the Teamster where he had just come from.

"I was filling in for the turbine crane operator, waiting to make a pick. I had been waiting for two hours and wasn't able to get anyone on the radio, so I came down to find a phone to call someone," the Teamster said

The ex-Marine ironworker apprentice laughed and said, "We hung two of those pricks out to dry over the railing."

Just then one of the three electricians peeked over the rail and said, "Hell, yeah! Two pricks just hanging around the turbine building."

The electrical foreman told the group they just smoked two fake guards in the relay room.

HELL FROM ABOVE

The ironworker foreman said they had a major problem on their hands. "We still have one of those assholes in that guard post at the edge of the turbine deck toward the river. We watched him kill the guard and pull his body into that booth."

One of the electricians added, "We're quite familiar with those guard post booths. When the three of us worked on the security upgrade project, we worked on those booths. The river outpost booths are equipped with 12-gauge shotguns, 9-mm pistols, gas masks, AR-15s and a .50-caliber Barrett rifle. If we all try and make a run for it, none of us will make it to the stairwell."

The Teamster said, "I got this; see that overhead crane?"

"The one that they're load testing?" the ironworker foreman asked.

The Teamster said, "Yes, the one that's suspending that five-thousand-pound load. I can sneak around the back, out of view of the booth, get into it, and crank up that bad boy's diesel, then turn the boom around, and hoover that load right over that booth. Someone can cause a distraction to get him out of the booth. I'm sure he won't go too far."

There were three large, empty wire reels in the work tent with them. The electrical foreman said, "We can roll the wheels across the turbine deck in his view, and when he comes out to see what's happening the Teamster can drop the load on his head."

The ex-MMA ironworker apprentice asked, "Whose 'we'?"

The electrical foreman replied, "We electricians. They're our wire reels, it's our work."

The whole group laughed.

One of the electricians asked, "What if he doesn't come out?"

The Teamster said laughingly, "Then we use the nuclear option. I hit the booth with that five-thousand-pound load that the crane is suspending until the booth goes over the edge of the turbine deck with dickhead still inside; problem solved. Besides, it's only held to the deck by four anchor bolts and the electricians installed them."

"Is that supposed to be funny?" one of the electricians said.

The Teamster successfully snuck into the crane's cab unnoticed. With a turn of the key and puff of black smoke, he started the crane's big diesel engine. He raised the boom and swung the load right above and in front of the guard booth.

The three electricians, who were still hiding behind the tent, began to roll one reel at a time into the view of the fake guard. After the third reel, the fake guard finally emerged from the booth, accidentally locking the door behind him. I could almost feel the whole gang think to themselves, "What an idiot."

The Teamster pulled the lever dropping the crane's load right on top of the idiot's head, as the Teamster shouted, "Here's your seventy-two virgins, bitch!"

HEADING TO THE RCA

Sunni had ordered four of his men to go to the radiation protection offices and take hostages. He told them if anyone resisted, don't hesitate to kill them. On the way to Rad Pro, the men passed through one of the open bay doors at the fire department. They shot two firefighters who were inside the garage recharging fire extinguishers and then proceeded to kill everyone in the office, including the fire chief. This was a damn shame since he was about to retire in one month. For all of his years of dedicated service, the company offered the beloved fire chief a cushy job in the nuclear training center post-retirement.

When Sunni's fake guards arrived at the Rad Pro offices, they went from room to room gathering anyone they could find and herding them into the locker room at gunpoint. They tie-wrapped their hands and duct-taped their mouths just like the warehouse workers, but left one fake guard to watch over them. One of the other fake guards went to the Rad Pro control point and commandeered the Rad Pro tech at his desk. His job is to sign personnel in and out of the radiation-controlled area (RCA). Since this area leads to the reactor containment hatch and other rooms that may contain radioactive components or contamination, entrance to this area is strictly controlled. The fake guard told the tech, "Any strange moves, I will kill you!"

Using two of the dead guard's access badges, the two fake guards entered the RCA and made their way to the fuel handling section of the building. Just down the hallway, where the fake guards would pass, was a room with a locked fence door where two nuke workers, two tool room attendants, and a Rad Pro supervisor were working. They were decontaminating and dose rating tools that two of the tool room attendants had just dropped off. All five suddenly became quiet as they heard the fake guards coming down the hallway laughing and speaking Arabic.

"What the hell kind of language is that?" asked one of the nuke workers.

A tool attendant whispered, "It's Arabic. I remember it from when I served in the gulf"

Without being noticed by the fake guards, the five watched them pass and agreed that none of them looked familiar.

"Who are they and why the hell are they dressed up like guards? And their carrying weapons?" said the other nuke worker.

Maggie, one of the nuke workers, said, "Are the force-on-force drills over?"

The other nuke worker, who was Maggie's older brother, said they had finished them over two days ago. Maggie, a tall, voluptuous brunette, had the pleasure of being partnered with her brother. Not everybody had the fortune—or misfortune (but not in this case)—of working with their kin. I always thought of Maggie as a sweet, kind girl. Whenever I crossed her path in the plant, I would tell her she was the prettiest girl there. In my opinion, she resembled the Native American Woman on the Land O

Lakes butter package. This particular day she was excited because the night before, the son of the control point entrance Rad Pro tech, currently being held hostage at gunpoint, had asked her to marry him.

DON'T MESS WITH HARRY

The Rad Pro tech supervisor in the room with them was Harry. He told the crew to stay put, while he went to the control point to see what was happening. Harry was a tall Army veteran loved by everyone in the Rad Pro department. If you wanted to get on Harry's good side, just talk about Harry's favorite subjects—basketball, apple pie, and fried chicken. Harry could put away some fried chicken. Poking his head outside the door to see if the fake guards were gone, he walked toward the door that led to the control point.

He looked through the little window of the control point Entrance door to see the entrance Rad Pro tech being shoved in the back of the head by a rifle as he sat at his desk. On the opposite side of the hallway where Harry ʼs standing, there was a phone on the wall. Harry picked the receiver and dialed Dave, the control point entrance ʼ. Harry watched as the guard prodded the tech with the for him to answer the phone. The tech finally answered ɔhone and said, "Control point, Dave speaking."

Harry said, "All good, Dave?"

ʼave answered, "Yes Bob, all good here, Bob!"

ɪst then, Dave looked up from his desk and made eye ct with Harry on the other side of the door. With a lown his spine, Harry then realized they all were in ʼrouble. Harry went back to the decontamination room to fill in the rest of the crew about the situation. Afterward, Harry locked the crew in a secure storage area across the hallway for their own protection, before leaving them to try and find help. He then entered one of the diesel generator rooms to use another phone. He felt safer there since this phone was located off the beaten path and hidden out of the way on a wall far in the back of the room. He tried calling the control room, security, fire department, but no one answered anywhere. Bad vibes coursed through him. When Harry wasn't supervising Rad Pro personnel, he was training Rad Pro techs in the processing center outside the gate.

Harry was very good friends with Little Jean, the plant psychiatrist's administration assistant. They had known each other for years. He tried calling her just as she was leaving for the day. "Jean, it's Harry, you don't know how glad I am you answered the phone."

Little Jean answered, "You're a lucky man, Harry, one more minute and you would have missed me. I am heading out for the day and, no, I don't have any more apple pie."

Harry said, "Jean, you need to get over to the sheriff's office and tell them the plant is being overrun by terrorists. They have taken over the control point, and Dave is being held hostage at gunpoint. I have no idea how many there are, but I do know, for sure, there are at least two guys dressed like our nuclear security guards somewhere here in the RCA. Don't waste any time. Quickly, GO!"

Little Jean went to the security office around the corner from her desk, then off to the medical office to sound the alarm only to find that everyone already had left for the day. Little Jean then hightailed it to the Possum County Sheriff's Office five miles down the road. Little Jean's premonition had come true. Her worst nightmare was coming to fruition, and she knew it was Youssef and Sunni.

Passing the main checkpoint on the access road, she considered telling the guard in the booth, but then had second thoughts remembering Harry saying the terrorists were dressed in nuclear security guard uniforms. She continued straight to the sheriff's office without stopping. Ironically, the guard at the checkpoint was a real guard and was phoning the security command center to find out where his night shift counterpart was.

"Command center, Lynn speaking."

"Lieutenant, this is Rudy at the checkpoint. My night shift officer hasn't arrived yet. It's been a half-hour and I'm on overtime now."

Lynn said, "Hey Fred, stay put until we can find you a replacement."

"Hey Fred? What's with the Fred stuff? I'm supposed to take my wife out to dinner for our anniversary."

Lynn said, "Sorry Fred, guess she'll have to take a raincheck."

After knowing Lynn for fifteen years, he couldn't figure out why she kept calling him Fred. Who's Fred, he thought.

Back in the control room, Youssef and his men were waiting for a call on the pager from the two men in the fuel handling section of the RCA letting them know they were in position and ready to die for Allah.

Meanwhile, Doreen ran from the service water building toward the water treatment building located about fifty yards away between the turbine building and the service water building on the river. She cautiously checked the building to see if it was occupied. Once she cleared the building, Doreen climbed a ladder to the rooftop by way of a trapdoor located in the ceiling of a maintenance room.

She looked around to find two fake guards on the roof of the service water building that she had just ran away from. She was extremely lucky those two fake guards had not seen her run from the building or she would have bought the farm for sure. Next to the service water building, she spotted two more fake guards on the roof of the circulating water building. She took a quick look behind, and then up, only to see the two fake guards the ironworkers had dangled by their feet up in the air over the guardrail against the outside wall of the turbine building. She also saw several familiar, smiling faces peeking over the top. They were the ironworkers, electricians and the Teamster all giving her the thumbs-up sign. She smiled as she motioned to them to get down. Doreen took a breath and thought about the situation. Knowing Doreen and her patriotic spirit, I always thought of her as possibly being a descendant of one of the trailblazing women who helped build this country in the 1800s Wild West. There was no choice between fight or flight with Doreen. She was in fight mode—and I'm glad I'm on her good side.

LITTLE JEAN VS.
STUBBORN SHERIFF

Meanwhile, Little Jean was at the Possum County Sheriff's Office desperately trying to convince the hardheaded sheriff and his deputies that this not a joke.

The sheriff told Little Jean, "We'll check it out, and you can go home now."

She replied, "No thanks, I'll wait here."

With a miserable look on his face, the sheriff told his two deputies to investigate. They both laughed and one said, "Terrorists, now that's a good one!"

Little Jean asked the sheriff if he was going to call anyone and if he wasn't, then he better let her borrow a phone and she would make the calls.

The sheriff said, "Hold tight, little girl, and wait until we hear back from Ted and Bill," his two deputies

Little Jean replied, "Dammit! You don't believe me."

He replied, "No reason to go off half-cocked now."

Deputies Ted and Bill stopped at the access road checkpoint and laughingly said to Rudy, "Hey, Rudy, we're here to investigate a terrorist takeover."

Rudy angrily replied, "I don't know about all that. I just know my replacement is an hour late, and it's my

66

20th wedding anniversary. I have dinner reservations in thirty minutes. I'm being forced to work overtime."

The deputies laughed and said, "No pussy for you for two weeks!"

As they drove off, Rudy flipped the two deputies the bird and said, "Go ahead and laugh, you dick's!"

The two deputies drove up to the security command center building.

Deputy Ted told Deputy Bill, "Wait here and let me check in, and we'll be back at the station before those Well burgers get cold."

Just then the sheriff asks Little Jean if she would like a world-famous Well burger.

Jean replied, "Stick it up your ass, pecker head!"

"Whoa!" the sheriff replied. "Okay, be that way, I was only trying to be hospitable, but that's okay. More for us."

As Deputy Bill was changing the radio station, Deputy Ted approached the building laughing to himself about the impossibility of a terrorist attack.

Just then, one of Sunni's men came out of the building and raised his rifle, shooting Deputy Ted dead right there on the steps. A panicked Deputy Bill shouted in the patrol car radio's microphone, "Deputy down, deputy down!"

The sheriff and Little Jean heard Deputy Bill's desperate cries for backup and then the sudden crackle of gunfire. After that, they heard nothing. The sheriff desperately shouted into the microphone, "Sheriff to Bill, Sheriff to Ted, come in!"

He then looked at Little Jean and said, "You really weren't kidding, were you?"

Little Jean replied, "No shit, genius!"

In a panic, the sheriff contacted the state police, marine police, and the local Coast Guard. The state police told the sheriff they were on the way with a SWAT team and the National Guard. Little Jean then suggested he call the NRC headquarters in Washington, DC. He told her that was a good idea. Little Jean replied, "I'm glad you approve, now get on the goddamn phone."

THE TURBINE TWO STEP

Back in the turbine building, Big Gary and I ducked into the now-abandoned Rad Pro break room. We peeked our heads into the locker room to find fifteen or more duct-taped hostages being held by an armed fake guard. Since the turbine building was attached to the auxiliary building, we decided to peek around the corner where we saw Rad Pro Dave being held at gunpoint at the RCA control point. We then decided it would be best to make our way to the turbine building's back stairwell and up to the roof to get a bird's-eye view of what was happening. When we got to the top deck, we ran around sea van containers and different types of equipment until we saw the work tent where the ironworkers, electricians, and the Teamster were hiding. We discussed the situation with them and decided the best thing to do was stay put. The gang said Doreen was on the roof of the water treatment plant below us and motioned for us to stay down. One of the electricians laughed and said, "Franny, peek your head out over the edge and tell me what you see."

As I peered over the edge of the roof, I laughed and said, "A couple of dangling rectums?"

The other electrician said, "Rectum? We damn near killed them."

I asked the group whether anyone had seen the millwrights, Greg, or Alphonse. Chris said he had seen all of them demobilizing equipment and gathering calibrated tools in the outer penetration building. That building is located outside of the turbine building and, as one of the electricians said, "They should be fine for a couple of hours. Besides, the bad guys have no interest in that part of the plant."

THE TERROR CONTINUES

n the control room, the operators, whose names I can't recall, nervously struggled to maintain the plant's operational status while two dead shift supervisors were lying on the floor. Just then, one of the two fake guards in the fuel handling spent fuel room, said loudly over the pager in Arabic, "Youssef, we're in position, praise be to Allah!"

Just then, the normally quiet and unremarkable spent fuel pool room suddenly became the most dangerous place in the plant.

Youssef grabbed the pager handset and told them to stand by. Harry, the Rad Pro supervisor, found two Rad Pro techs in the truck bay not far below the floor where the men that just paged Youssef. These two Rad Pro techs had been performing radiological surveys unaware and undetected by the evil men in the room just above them. Harry saw the techs and motioned to them to keep quiet.

Meanwhile, back on top of the water treatment plant roof, Doreen spotted two military-style patrol boats heading toward the circulating water and service water intake structure buildings.

The fake guards on the service water building began shooting at the oncoming boats. What a fatal mistake.

Doreen was perched on the roof of the water treatment building in clear view of the two fake guards who were on the roof of the service water building. She aimed carefully and, with two quick, accurate shots, fired her rifle, taking out both fake guards. Just then a loud "brrrrr," could be heard as the gunner on the Coast Guard patrol boat took out both fake guards on top of the circulating water building.

Far across the plant property, one of the bad guys on the roof of the warehouse had witnessed the gun battle by the river and rushed to a plant pager shouting, "Youssef, Youssef, military patrol boats coming onto site, many men, soldiers, helicopters."

Armored personnel carriers, state police SWAT teams, and swarms of men from the Possum County Sheriff's Office Tactical Team sped by Rudy, the confused access checkpoint guard. He remembered saying to himself, "I'm never going to go to dinner tonight!"

Half of a police SWAT team had headed toward the warehouse while the other half went to the security center. The sheriff's tactical teams gathered in the now-vacant processing center. Helicopters circled the warehouse and security center.

The two fake guards on the roof of the warehouse had opened fire on a Black Hawk chopper. The helicopter returned fire instantly and took out the two bad guys with a quick burst from its 20-mm Vulcan gun.

Just as the Coast Guard and state police patrol boats were tying up to the service water structure, Doreen waved her hands and yelled frantically, "Don't shoot!" as she unlocked the gate to the river allowing the Special Operations teams entrance to the plant yard. She filled in the team leaders of both the Coast Guard and the state police about the situation as best she knew. She told them her lieutenant and best friend, Lynn, was being held hostage in the command center by the terrorists.

The team leaders radioed in the new information to the other Special Operations teams. A chopper dropped a Delta Force anti-terrorist team on the roof of the warehouse by rope and the other chopper landed in the lot of the security center. Meanwhile, a third helicopter dropped another Special Ops team on the roof of the turbine building after getting an all-clear sign from the workers hiding on the roof below.

TRUE HEROES

In the control room, Youssef screamed to one of the operators to shut down all four of the spent fuel cooling pumps. The operator said, "I can't, you'll put us into ORAM RED. We'll only have twelve minutes before the spent fuel pool will start to boil, creating a hydrogen cloud to form and eventually igniting a Chernobyl-like situation."

Youssef screamed, "Shut them down now!"

The operator said, "We'll kill 10,000 people when it blows, and none of us will make it out of here alive. The radiation will kill us all."

Youssef grabbed one of the fake guard's rifles and shot the operator. He then put the rifle to another operator's head as he walked him over to the control room panel board. The operator snapped one switch. As the annunciator board lit up, sirens and lights began to alarm. Youssef screamed! "All of them…Now!"

Reluctantly, the operator snapped the other three switches as the rest of the board lights started blinking rapidly. After the last switch was snapped, Youssef killed the operator.

The four remaining control room personnel eyed Youssef nervously as he told the fake guards in Arabic, "Don't kill them yet, we may need them."

Back in the fuel handling area, Harry and the two Rad Pro techs agreed they had to do something quickly. They realized close to 10,000 lives or more might be in peril. They were aware time was of the essence, when the three of them heard all four spent fuel cooling pumps stop running. There's a 480-volt temporary power cable feeding a trans panel that controlled the lights at the spent fuel pool where the men were. Harry and the Rad Pro techs peeked over the top of the stairs to find the men staring at the spent fuel pool with their backs to them.

One fake guard had the pager in his hand and said to Youseff in Arabic, "Steam is coming off the pool now."

Just then Harry tripped the main breaker on the trans panel shutting off the lights to the spent fuel pool room above, as the two Rad Pro techs rushed the fake guards. Harry saw many muzzle flashes as the techs struggled with the fake guards. One of the techs grabbed a fake guard's rifle and shot both guards and accidentally clipped his partner in the leg. Just then Harry turned the lights on and yelled, "All clear?"

Both techs yelled back, "All clear!" Harry yelled into the plant pager, which was set to the control room channel, "One Control, One Control. We need you to get those pumps back up quickly. NOW!"

THE CAVALRY ARRIVES

One member of the Army's Special Operations team made his way to the outside corridor of the control room. An in-house maintenance chief named Joe briefed the Special Ops team leader on the control room layout. He told them the control room is pressurized and if they tossed a smoke grenade or tear gas canister into the ventilation duct in the hallway, within sixty seconds the control room would be obscured by the gas and smoke.

Once again, the occupants in the control room heard Harry yelling frantically over the pager, "The water is starting to boil, get those pumps up now or it will be too late!"

As Youssef heard Harry, he told the other fake guard, "If anyone moves toward the control panel board, kill them!"

Outside of the control room in the hallway, the Special Ops team removed the vent grating and tossed a smoke grenade and tear gas canister into the ventilation duct just as Joe had suggested. Within a minute the entire control room was filled with choking smoke and gas.

Out of the four men Youseff's fake guard was watching, three of them were fresh out of the military. They had just been discharged from the Navy's elite Silent Submarine Service with honors. Submarine operators are highly trained to work in toxic and smoky environments. Within a minute, the smoke and gas caught Youseff and the fake guard by surprise. In the dense smoke, one of the operators dropped to the floor crawling toward the control room door allowing entry to the gas mask-wearing Special Ops team. The other two grabbed Youseff while disarming his fake guard by knocking him to the ground with his own rifle. The other operator made his way to the control room panel board snapping all four cooling pump switches back to the "on" position. Quickly, the Special Ops team led the four operators to the hallway and fresh air. The team leader and another Special Ops member grabbed Youssef and dragged his fake guard to the hallway coughing and gagging profusely while screaming, "Die Infidels!"

Another assault team easily took out all of the fake guards in the security center and the remaining fake guards outside of the command center bunker.

Still inside the bunker, Sunni and his fake guard must have felt like Custer at Little Big Horn. However, they still held Lynn and another real guard hostage in the heavily secured room.

Back in the Rad Pro office area, another assault team split up taking out control point tech Dave's fake guard at the check-in desk and the fake guard watching over the hostages in the Rad Pro locker room. The team that was dropped by line from the chopper above the warehouse quickly took control, killing all of the fake guards and freeing the hostages without any injuries.

Doreen rushed with the SWAT team toward the security center where her bestie, Lynn, was being held by Sunni and another fake guard. When they arrived, a SWAT team member said to the leader, "All secured but the command center bunker."

The plant manager, who had not arrived yet on site, had declared an "unusual event" after being notified by the

Possum County sheriff. The manager then activated the emergency response team, which consisted of engineers, security personnel, senior nuclear shift operators, maintenance staff, and equipment operators. When on call, they would leave their homes at a moment's notice and head to the plant. Once they arrived on site, they waited for the all-clear command so they could take over and ensure the plant would continue operating safely.

PROCEED TO YOUR
ACCOUNTABILITY AREA

Since all but two of the terrorists had been neutralized and a hostage situation still remained, an announcement had been put across the plant paging system by the manager saying the plant was "not back in a safe condition yet" and anyone who had been on-site while these events occurred were to report immediately to their accountability area as per procedure, only if safe to do so. In our case, the cafeteria was our muster area. Arriving there, we ran in to Alphonse, Greg and both millwright general foreman at the vending machines getting snacks.

Alphonse said to me, "How's tricks, Franny?"

I replied, "Do any of you guys have a clue as to what's been going on around here all day?"

Greg said, "No, we've been cooped up in one of the outer penetration rooms all day rounding up equipment, but I'm sure you're going to tell us."

Just then the electrician foreman told the clueless men, "Sit in the truck, and don't touch the radio." These guys had no idea what had been unfolding around them throughout the day.

WE DON'T MAKE DEALS
WITH TERRORISTS

———————

Back at the security center, an FBI hostage negotiator had just arrived and was talking to Sunni on the phone. In the meantime, SWAT snipers had taken positions on the roof of the nearby buildings. Sunni demanded that the negotiator provide him and his fake guard with a chopper to take them to a hangar where a private jet would fly them to a location in the Middle East. If their demands were met, they would release the hostages at the airport. The hostage negotiator told Sunni the President assured him and his guard safe passage back to the Middle East only if the hostages were kept alive and unharmed.

A SWAT team leader radioed to all of his men in the building to vacate immediately as a chopper landed in the yard. On the camera monitors Lynn controlled, Sunni watched the team leave the building as a chopper landed in the yard. Just then, the negotiator called Sunni to tell him "All was a go!"

All four emerged from the security center in a tight formation with Sunni holding Lynn's 9-mm pistol to her head while the fake guard held his pistol against the real guard's head. Fearing she might lose Lynn, her best friend, Doreen asked the SWAT team leader how they intended to get them free when they got to the airport. Just then two of the rooftop snipers radioed in, "all clear!"

After being distracted, the SWAT team leader asked Doreen, "What airport? This isn't the movies, this is real."

The team leader radioed back to his snipers, "You have permission to fire when clear!"

As the group moved toward the chopper, over the noise of the blades Doreen heard two loud pops. Both Sunni and his fake guard were shot dead. Doreen, Lynn, and the real guard were white as ghosts. All three were speechless as Doreen rushed to join the two in a group hug.

The SWAT team leader radioed, "All targets neutralized. Great job, team! Head back to base for a debrief and cocktails."

EPILOGUE

<hr />

I t had been a long day. Per procedure, all plant personnel involved in the day's events were told to go to their
designated accountability stations for a head count. We
were all told that a Nuclear Regulatory Commission team
from Washington, DC, would be arriving at the plant the
next day to interview everyone individually about what
had occurred.

The next day, a large group gathered and waited outside
a big meeting room in the administration building for what
seemed like hours. One by one, each person went into the
conference room. One by one, each person emerged with a
strange look on their face, only to be asked by co-workers,
"What did they ask you?" Everyone who had entered that
meeting room had the same response, "We're not allowed
to discuss it."

Then, a pipefitter foreman named John who happened
to be on-site that day in a remote area of the plant and was
unaware of the happenings remarked, "What the hell? Are
we in Russia?"

When John came out of the room, I asked him, "What
happened, John?"

With an angry look on his face, he said, "Can't discuss it!"

The Well was busy that afternoon. It seemed as though
everyone who attended the NRC interviews met at the bar

afterward to compare notes. Sitting at two tables pushed together was the regular gang plus Greg, both millwright foremen, John the pipefitter, Alphonse, me, and Timmy "WTF."

Doreen and Lynn arrived at our table a couple of minutes later. Lynn asked the group, "Has anyone seen today's paper? The plant manager said an 'unusual event' had occurred. The plant spokesperson would not specify the details. But he did remark that all is back to normal and at no time was the public in danger!"

Timmy "WTF" said, "Tell it to the families that lost their relatives."

One of the millwrights said, "Really. How are they going to explain that?"

Alphonse chimed in, "Dats a simple, Dey won't."

Changing the subject, I said, "Let's have a toast to our heroes. Here, here, to Little Jean, Doreen, Lynn, our union ironworkers, electricians, and even the Teamster!"

Little Jean said, "Don't forget Harry, and the two Rad Pro techs."

We all raised our glasses, "Salut."

Just then Doreen asked, "Are those two assholes still hanging off the side of the turbine building?"

Some guy at the table next to us laughed and said, "Just before the SWAT team cut them down, we saw the Teamster hang one of the ironworkers' topping-off flags over them."

With a beer in hand, the ironworker foreman turned around in his stool at the bar and said, "Yeah, and we better get our damn flag back."

Alphonse said, "A toasta to oura brave departed. Salut!"

This would be the last time we ever discussed the events that were touted by the press and the plant manager as a non-dangerous situation.

Acknowledgements

In the summer of 1980 before to heading off to college, I had the opportunity of a lifetime. IBEW (International Brotherhood of Electrical Workers) Local 592 in Vineland, New Jersey, was offering a summer work program. Members' children who were eighteen and older were eligible. They would be working with the members at various construction sites within their territory.

My father, Tom Curry, a proud IBEW member, asked me if I was interested. I jumped at the opportunity and was assigned to work for the Bechtel Corporation during the construction of the Hope Creek Nuclear Power Plant Reactor No. 2, Lower Alloways Creek, New Jersey. The rest is history.

Twenty-eight years later, I can tell you it has been an interesting, wild ride. Words cannot express the profound feelings of fear and curiosity, along with the smell and sounds of entering a nuclear reactor containment hatch for the first time while the unit is under full power. The musty smell and echoing, pinging sound of the neutron detector (an alarm goes off if there's a neutron release) gives you the distinct impression of what it must be like in a submarine.

I would like to thank all the people I worked with and around all those years. They are like one big family.

I am grateful to my friends who shared their time and experiences with me. I am also blessed to live on Fripp Island, a barrier island located off the coast of South Carolina where the spirits of several writers past and present have entered my soul.

Thank you, Dr. Mary Thornton Jacobs for encouraging me to tell my story. Mary is one of many Fripp Island authors. She is well-known for her leadership books and the "Big Daddy Raccoon on Fripp Island" series of children books. There are too many people who have influenced me over the years to mention, so please forgive me if I didn't call out everyone. You know who you are.

End Notes / Glossary

Barney Fife: Bernard "Barney" Fife is a fictional character in the American television program The Andy Griffith Show, portrayed by comic actor Don Knotts. Barney Fife is a high-strung deputy sheriff in the slow-paced, sleepy southern community of Mayberry, North Carolina

Barrett rifle: A high powered semi-automatic or bolt action .50 caliber rifle

Baymen: Commercial Fishermen/women, Crabbers, and Oyster harvesters on the Delaware Bay.

BWR (Boiling Water Reactor): A boiling water reactor is a type of light water nuclear reactor used for the generation of electrical power. It is the second most common type of electricity-generating nuclear reactor after the pressurized water reactor, his is also a type of light water nuclear reactor.

CFCU: Containment fan coil units are large ventilation units that provide temperature control with-in a containment building.

Controlled Burning: Setting planned fires to maintain the health of the marsh grassed.

Cooling tower: A cooling tower is a special heat exchanger in which air and water are brought into direct contact with each other in order to reduce the water's temperature. As this occurs, a small volume of water is evaporated, reducing the temperature of the water being circulated through the tower.

DCP: Design Change Packages are engineered work packages that change or modify the configuration of a component or system.

Demobing: The job of taking down and storing equipment, cords, and anything temporarily related for the support of a plant shutdown.

ELSA Pack: Emergency Life Saving Apparatus is an escape hood with an oxygen tank to be worn during a fire or lack of oxygen. Their use is limited to the amount of oxygen in the tank. Originally designed for ships crews to escape to safety in the event of a fire or lack of oxygen.

Farmette: Farmette or "Hobby Farm" is a small residential farm run by an owner who earns income from a source other than the farm. Generally a farmette owner would have some livestock and outbuildings as well.

FFD: Fitness for duty testing of personnel. Random selection of personnel to test for alcohol or drug use. For Cause testing is done when personnel have been involved in an accident, or when there is suspicion the employee may be under the influence of drugs or alcohol.

500 KV: 500,000 volts

FME: Foreign Material Exclusion is the process of preventing the introduction of outside debris into an area or areas that debris poses an economic risk or safety hazard. It is widely used in the nuclear generation community as an attempt to increase nuclear safety and reduce power plant down time.

Foreman: A worker who supervises and directs other workers.

General Foreman: Sometimes known as a site supervisor or construction works manager, is responsible for general management, organizational and operational control of a construction site.

Hole Watch: A trained confined space attendant responsible for the safety of personnel working with in a confined space.

HP or Rad Pro Tech: Health Physics technicians or Radiation Protection technicians are highly trained safety technicians that ensure workplace safety in industries that use radioactive materials or expose people to radioactivity sources.

IBEW: International Brotherhood of Electrical Workers is a labor union that represents nearly 750,00 workers and retirees in the electrical industry in the United States, Canada, Panama, Guam, and several Caribbean island states.

INC Technicians: They are highly skilled technicians trained in instrument calibration and testing.

Island 500: A slang term for the daily race home during the construction phase of the fictional "Triumph" nuclear plant. A daily race between hundreds of cars to get off the island at quitting time.

Laborer: Construction and demolition workers.

MOV's: Motorized Operated valves. Usually computer controlled, but can be operated manually.

NRC: Nuclear Regulatory Commission- Is an independent agency of the United States government tasked with protecting public health and safety related to nuclear energy. Operating Engineer Heavy equipment operators such as, but not limited cranes, fork lifts and such.

Pipe Fitter: Install and maintain pipes that carry chemicals, acids, and gases. These pipes are used mostly in manufacturing, commercial and industrial settings.

Teamster: Truck driver.

TP&L: Temporary Power and Lighting.

RCA: Radiation controlled area is a zone established for the controlling movement of radiation sources and personnel.

Woodshed: A slang term for the electrical General Foreman's office.